Erin stood transfixed in horror. She'd been right after all! Somebody *had* been in the house—somebody had been in that very room, carefully removing the picture of Abby and Mr. Peters and then systematically destroying it.

Her mind raced. Who could it have been? Why would anyone do such a thing? She couldn't think of any rational reason. And the weirdest part of it was that nothing else in the house had been disturbed. She sank into the desk chair, trembling as a wave of fear washed over her. What was going on?

BEVERLY HASTINGS divides her time between New York and California. *WATCHER IN THE DARK* is her first book for young adults.

WATCHER IN THE DARK

BEVERLY HASTINGS

BERKLEY BOOKS, NEW YORK

WATCHER IN THE DARK

A Berkley Book/published by arrangement with
the authors

PRINTING HISTORY
Berkley/Pacer edition / April 1986
Berkley edition / April 1991

ISBN: 0-425-10131-2
RL: 6.1

A BERKLEY BOOK ® TM 757,375
Berkley Books are published by The Berkley Publishing Group,
200 Madison Avenue, New York, New York 10016.
The name "BERKLEY" and the "B" logo
are trademarks belonging to Berkley Publishing Corporation.

10 9 8 7 6

CHAPTER ONE

Erin yanked the back door open and rushed across the kitchen to the phone that still rang insistently. "Hello?" she said breathlessly. "Peters residence."

No one spoke at the other end of the line. "Hello?" Erin said again. Listening, she thought, I know there's someone there, I can hear breathing. "Hello," she said into the phone once more. "Who's calling?"

The faint sound of breathing continued for a moment longer, and then there was a definite click as the caller hung up.

Erin shivered. The caller had no doubt simply dialed a wrong number and hadn't been polite enough to apologize. Still, the call gave her a creepy feeling. It was unnerving to know that someone at the other end was just listening in silence.

With an impatient gesture, Erin pushed her straight black hair behind her ears and then headed for the door. She went outside again into the backyard.

Abby, the little girl Erin was baby-sitting for, was still sitting on the swing, but by now it had slowed to a gentle rocking motion. "Want me to push you some more?" Erin asked.

"No, I'm tired of swinging." Abby jumped off and stood in front of Erin, peering hopefully up at her. "Could we go get frozen yogurt?"

Erin laughed. "It's not summer yet, Abby."

"I know," the little girl said seriously, "but I'm hot."

Glancing at her watch, Erin thought, Oh, why not? It's early enough so a treat won't spoil her dinner. Aloud she said, "Okay, we'll walk down to the Soda Shoppe." She smiled at Abby's squeal of delight and added, "Do you know what flavor you want?"

As they walked from Abby's house toward the row of shops that made up Wentworth's downtown, Abby continued to ponder which kind of frozen yogurt would be best for this first one of the season. She had just about made up her mind to try raspberry when they walked into the little soda fountain, but at the last minute she hesitated. "Would I like peach better?" she asked Erin.

"How about if we get one of each and share them?" Erin suggested.

Soon they were outside again in the spring sunshine. They ambled slowly along the street, looking at the displays in the store windows. Abby was staring longingly at a collection of plush Easter bunnies when Erin heard a familiar voice behind them.

"Well, look who's here—the beautiful and charming Erin Moore! Sure looks like you're starting your spring vacation with a bang, Erin."

His tone was mocking and Erin felt herself stiffen as she turned to face Greg Brockton. Why couldn't he just leave her alone? It was all over between them—surely she'd made that plain enough to him. But he acted as if he didn't believe she really meant it.

Keeping the annoyance out of her voice, Erin said, "It's as good a start as any."

Greg smiled at her without speaking, and Erin's cheeks flushed. He'd always been able to make her feel a little foolish, and Erin knew he was making fun of her. But if that's the way he feels, why does he act as if he's still interested in me? she thought almost angrily. He's so gorgeous, he could have any girl he wants. Why bother with me?

Before she could come up with anything clever to say, Greg reached out and closed his strong hand around hers. With an easy familiarity, he leaned closer and slurped up a mouthful of her frozen yogurt.

"I didn't know you were going to be around this week," he said. "Guess I'll be seeing you at Jimmy Randall's big bash tomorrow night, huh? And if you're lucky, I might even drive you home afterward."

"I won't be there," Erin said. "I'm going to be staying at Abby's house, taking care of her all week while her dad is out of town."

Greg shook his head. "Well, I guess that tells me where I stand—beaten out by a little kid." He was smiling, but his blue eyes were cold as he stared at Erin. Then he put his hand lightly on Abby's blond curls. "Have fun." Reaching out to touch Erin's cheek, he added, "See you 'round." He turned on his heel and strode away down the sidewalk, the angry set of his shoulders revealing the temper he barely held in check.

Erin felt a chill down her spine as she took Abby's hand. Who did Greg think he was, assuming that she'd drop everything to go to Jimmy's party with him? When would he get it through his head that she wasn't interested in him anymore?

Annoyed with Greg and also with herself, Erin thought, I shouldn't have even explained why I wasn't going tomorrow night. What I should have said was that I wouldn't go home with Greg now if he were the last person on earth.

Exasperated, she pushed her hair back from her face. When they reached the house, Abby was tired from the walk. After Erin had helped her wipe her sticky mouth and fingers, Abby asked, "Can I watch TV until my dad gets home?"

When Erin nodded, the child ran into the living room and curled up on the couch with her teddy bear. Turning on *Sesame Street*, Erin sat down beside her.

Soon they heard a car pull into the driveway. "Daddy's home!" the little girl cried, and a moment later Mr. Peters entered the house.

"How's my favorite girl?" Mr. Peters asked as he swung Abby up in his arms and hugged her. "Now I need to talk to Erin for a minute," he said. "Remember, I told you I have to go away on a business trip, and Erin's going to stay here with you while I'm gone." Abby nodded and he continued, "You two girls are going to be in charge of each other after I leave tomorrow.''

As Erin followed him into his study, Mr. Peters asked, ''Now is there anything I've forgotten to tell you?''

''I don't think so,'' she replied. There wasn't much Erin didn't already know about the Peters household. She'd been sitting for Abby three afternoons a week for more than a year. Abby went to nursery school every morning and was picked up by Mrs. Grey, a retired schoolteacher, at noon. On Tuesdays and Thursdays the little girl stayed at Mrs. Grey's house until about six when her father came to get her. But Mr. Peters felt that his daughter needed a younger, more energetic person to take care of her at least part of the time. He'd hired Erin for the other three afternoons and sometimes, if he was late getting home from the office, Erin stayed on to feed Abby and put her to bed. ''I think I pretty much know Abby's routines by now,'' she told him.

''I'm sure you do,'' he replied. ''Now, let me show you—I've put my itinerary here on my desk, just in case you need to get in touch with me.'' Giving her a reassuring smile, he went on, ''But I don't expect that anything will happen with a conscientious girl like you in charge. So we're all set, right? I'll see you tomorrow morning at nine o'clock.''

Erin returned his smile. "Right," she replied. Calling good-bye to Abby, she left the house and started toward her own home.

As she walked along in the fading light, Erin thought about the week ahead. She was flattered that Mr. Peters trusted her to take total charge of his daughter while he was gone and she was excited at the idea of being on her own. Of course her own parents would be at home and available if she needed anything while she was living in the Peters house, but Mr. Peters himself would be thousands of miles away.

This job over Easter break would be a nice change of pace, and Erin certainly wouldn't mind the extra money she'd be making. She'd been so bored with school lately—it was good to have something else to think about. It wasn't that she didn't enjoy her classes—they were fine and she had fun working on the school newspaper. But she'd been going to school with the same bunch of kids for almost twelve years now, and she was ready for a change.

Erin laughed wryly at herself. Who was she trying to kid? The main reason she'd be glad for her senior year to end was that when it was over, she wouldn't be running into Greg anymore.

She sighed, feeling a little sorry for herself. She and Greg had gone together since almost the beginning of the school year and now that they'd split up, Erin had to admit that it wasn't so easy. She'd gotten used to being half of an established couple and even though she really didn't like him anymore, it was kind of lonely without a boyfriend.

As she let herself into her house, she couldn't shake off the memory of Greg's sneering smile and the bitterness in his voice.

Maybe I imagined it, she thought. But no matter how she tried to tell herself that everything was all right, she knew it wasn't true.

CHAPTER TWO

When Erin arrived the next morning, Mr. Peters was all ready to leave for the airport. "Don't forget that there's a spare key to the house hidden in the garage," he told Erin. "You know where it is, don't you? And here's the key to the car—it's all filled with gas. Of course you know where the phone numbers for the doctor and everything are, right?"

Erin assured him that she did. "Everything's going to be fine, Mr. Peters. Abby and I are going to have a great time while you're gone."

The cab pulled up in front and, with a final hug for Abby, Mr. Peters was off.

Abby looked a bit forlorn as she sat in the front window with her teddy bear, gazing after the departing cab. Wanting to distract her, Erin said, "Why don't we get out your crayons and

some paper? You can draw a picture of your
dad, and we'll hang it up on the wall in your
room.''

The little girl considered for a moment and
then went into her father's study. On the book-
shelf was a silver-framed photograph of herself
and her father, laughing into the camera. She
brought it into the dining room where Erin had
set out paper and crayons on the table. ''I'm
going to make the exact same picture,'' she told
Erin, and soon she was bent in fierce concentration over the paper.

When she had finished her portrait, she held
it up for Erin to admire. Then she asked, ''Aren't
you going to make a picture, Erin?''

''Sure,'' the older girl said. ''I know—let's
make a big picture of the flowers in the garden.
We'll work on it together.''

The child nodded. ''Okay.'' On a clean sheet
of paper she carefully began filling in a narrow
strip of green across the botton. ''This is the
grass,'' she informed Erin.

''I know,'' Erin said, suppressing a smile and
remembering all the similar pictures she had
made herself as a small child. They had hung
for ages on the kitchen wall at home.

The phone rang as Abby carefully drew in a
bright purple flower. ''Go ahead,'' Erin told her
as she moved toward the kitchen. She wondered

if this was Mr. Peters calling to give her some last-minute instructions. Looking around for a pencil in case she needed one, she picked up the receiver. "Peters residence."

For a moment she thought it was a bad connection, but then she heard the faint sound of someone breathing on the open line. Not again! she thought, annoyed. "Hello?" she said loudly. "Who is this?" Just as before, she heard the decisive click as the caller hung up.

"Who was it?" Abby wanted to know when Erin returned to the table.

"Nobody," Erin told her. "Whoever it was just hung up."

"Oh," Abby said without interest, and went back to the tree she was adding to the picture. But as Erin began drawing a row of red tulips, she wondered who it could be that was calling the Peters house. It couldn't simply be a wrong number—the person would have said something when it happened two days in a row. But whoever's calling just sits there listening and doesn't say a word.

There was really nothing to be afraid of in these calls, Erin knew, but still they were beginning to make her nervous. Come on, she scolded herself silently, don't start scaring yourself about something so ridiculous.

Around noon the two of them set out for Erin's house. It was nice of Mom to think of inviting Abby to lunch, Erin reflected. I know she didn't want her to feel lonely this first day of her dad's trip. Then Erin smiled to herself. I bet her real reason is to make sure I'm doing okay—sometimes Mom doesn't seem to realize that I can handle things on my own.

When they got there, Abby greeted Erin's parents politely. She was obviously longing to see Erin's own room, however, and the two of them went upstairs. The little girl was fascinated with the assortment of bottles that stood on a little tray. Fingering the clear nail polish, she asked, "Will you fix my nails like yours, Erin?"

Thinking that lunch wasn't too far off, Erin said, "Not this time. But you can use some cologne. Smell these and see which one you like best."

A moment later Mrs. Moore called up the stairs to say that lunch was ready, and the two girls went down to the dining room. During the meal Abby chattered merrily in response to Erin's parents' questions, and Erin realized that it had been a long time since they'd had a little girl at their table. She noticed, too, that her mom had made an effort to provide the kind of meal a four-year-old would appreciate—hot dogs on buns wasn't what they usually had for Saturday lunch at home.

When they'd finished, Erin's dad pushed back his chair and announced that he was going out to feed the birds.

"What do you feed them?" Abby asked.

He smiled at her. "Why don't you come and help me fill the bird feeders and then you can see for yourself?"

As Abby scrambled out of her chair and eagerly trotted off with him, Erin's mother asked, "So, tell me, how's everything going?"

"Mom, I only started this morning," Erin protested.

Her mother smiled. "I know. But it's so quiet around here with you and Sean both gone."

"We'll both be back soon, Mom," Erin pointed out. After all, she thought, her fourteen-year-old brother was only away for a ski week in Canada and Erin herself was practically around the corner. How was her mother going to feel next September when she went off to college?

"I ran into Marge Brockton this morning in the supermarket," her mother was saying. "She asked how you were and said she was sorry that you wouldn't be going to the prom with Greg." Erin said nothing, and her mother went on, "I could tell she was just fishing, so I told her that you hadn't decided who you wanted to go with yet.''

Erin's laugh sounded hollow. She wasn't sure anyone was going to ask her, but her mother seemed to really believe that thousands of guys were standing in line. She wondered what else Greg's mother had wanted to find out.

"You know, Erin," her mother continued, "I'm not sorry you decided to stop seeing Greg. I didn't want to say so before, but I never thought he was the boy for you.''

"Well, you were right," Erin said lightly. But not for the reasons I told you, she thought. Her mom felt Greg was conceited. Good-looking, state diving champion, honor student—you name it, Greg Brockton had it and he certainly knew it. But that wasn't what had been too much for Erin in the end. "I wish Becky were here.''

Her mom looked at her in surprise and Erin realized she'd spoken her thought out loud. Becky, her best friend since fourth grade, was the only one who knew the real story about Greg.

"But, honey, you know how much Becky's family was looking forward to their trip to Virginia. She'll be back before you know it. You girls only have a week of spring break, after all. I'm sure you can manage being apart that long," Erin's mother said with a little laugh. "And that reminds me—Jill Saunders called this morning and she wanted you to call her back.''

Before Erin could reply, Abby burst into the room. ''It's so neat. I got to put the seeds into the feeder, and as soon as I was done a bunch of birds came and started eating. They must have been hungry!''

Abby joined in the general laughter, but Erin noticed that the little girl's eyelids were beginning to droop. Poor kid, she'd probably been up since the crack of dawn watching her dad pack for his trip. ''Come on, Abby, time to go home,'' Erin said gently.

''Now, Erin, you just call if you need anything at all,'' her mother said earnestly. ''We'll be right here.''

''Sure, Mom, I will. Now, Abby, let's find your—''

''Oh, dear,'' Erin's mother broke in. ''I'd forgotten that we promised Guy and Elaine we'd drive up and have dinner with them—they've found some new place they want us to try.'' Mrs. Moore glanced worriedly at her husband. ''I don't know, honey, do you think—''

Impatiently Erin cut in. ''Honestly, Mom, don't worry. We'll be fine.''

By the time they'd reached the Peters house, Abby made no objection when Erin suggested a nap. They found her teddy bear where she'd left him on the window seat. Then Erin tucked the two of them snugly in the child's bed and tiptoed down the stairs.

Remembering her mom's message, she picked up the phone and dialed Jill Saunders's number. "Hi, Jill, it's Erin."

"Oh, hi, how're you doing? I just wanted to make sure you knew about Jimmy Randall's party tonight. I think it starts around eight, so—"

"Yeah, I heard about it," Erin broke in, "but I'm not going."

"You're kidding! It's going to be great. Everyone will be there, and Jimmy's parents are going out. Why don't you want to go?"

Erin explained that she was baby-sitting for Abby, and Jill replied impatiently, "But that's silly. Just get someone else to stay with the kid for the evening. Let's see—I bet Bruce's younger sister would do it."

"Thanks, Jill, but I don't think so."

After a pause, Jill said, "I get it—you don't want to run into Greg. But, Erin, I don't understand what's happening between you two."

"Nothing," Erin told her shortly. "That's the point."

"Come on, aren't you guys going to get back together?"

"I don't think so." Erin didn't really want to

discuss this with Jill, especially since Jill's boy-friend, Bruce, was Greg's best friend.

"Really?" Jill sighed. "Well, I guess you know what you're doing. But I can't figure out what went wrong with you two. I mean, I thought you were the perfect couple." She paused expectantly, but when Erin didn't respond, she went on, "I guess I was wrong, though. Anyway, I wish you'd change your mind about tonight. You could come with me and Bruce."

"Thanks for the offer," Erin said, "but I'm definitely not going."

After saying good-bye, Erin settled on the couch with her book. It was one she needed to read for a report before the end of the school year, and she'd decided she might as well get going on it. When the phone rang, she leaped to answer it so that it wouldn't awaken Abby.

She snatched up the receiver. "Hello. Peters residence," she said softly. Several seconds went by and there was no response on the other end of the line. "Hello?" Erin said a little louder and then waited a second or two more. "Listen, whoever you are—" She heard the indrawn breath of surprise but still there was no other response.

Angry now, Erin said bitingly, "Look, I'm tired of this. I don't know what stupid game you're playing but just cut it out! Don't call here anymore.'' She replaced the receiver abruptly, and for a moment she enjoyed the satisfaction that at least this time she'd been the one to hang up first.

Then she wondered, had she done the right thing? She'd always read that when you got obscene phone calls, the thing to do was to hang up without uttering a word. Should she have handled this silent listener the same way? Maybe her response was just what he'd wanted.

But what kind of person could get a thrill out of listening to her get annoyed? It didn't seem very exciting. Then a new and alarming idea struck her. Maybe this was a burglar, calling the house to find out if it was empty. When he heard a real person speaking and could tell it wasn't an answering machine, he'd just hang up. Then he'd keep trying, waiting for the uninterrupted ringing that would tell him no one was home.

Erin shivered and wished she hadn't thought of this possibility. The feeling that some unknown person out there was watching her or keeping tabs on what she did was really spooky.

A gust of wind rattled the panes in the living room windows as Erin returned to the couch. She jumped at the noise and then, as she picked up her book, she noticed that her hands were shaking. Stop it, she told herself. Don't let your imagination run away with you. And even if it is a potential burglar calling, the whole reason he does it is to find out if I'm home—he won't try anything while I'm here.

Trying to hang on to this comforting thought, Erin opened her book. But after several minutes of turning the pages, she found herself unable to concentrate on it. The house was awfully quiet and finally Erin realized that she was unused to being so alone. At home she had her parents and her younger brother Sean around, and she also spent a lot of time with Becky. It seemed as though they were always in and out of one another's houses. And of course, for most of this year, she'd been with Greg.

She put down her book and stared into space. A lot of people thought she'd been a fool to stop seeing him. Jill Saunders had come right out and said so.

When Erin had first started going out with Greg, she couldn't believe her luck. He was definitely the best-looking boy in the class and he seemed to be good at everything without even trying. She remembered the first time they'd gone out together and how smug she'd felt when they'd walked into Casey's. Lots of the girls would have gladly traded places with her.

At first Erin had been in such a glow—everything had seemed perfect to her. Only gradually had she realized that, though he always asked for her opinion or advice, he only heard it when it agreed with his own. And even then, he was so much fun to be with that she'd closed her eyes to the biting sarcasm in his comments about other people. His jokes had often verged on cruelty, and Greg seemed to have a knack for finding someone's weak spots.

Erin shuddered, remembering how terrible she'd felt when she heard that Hugh Wallace had tried to kill himself. He was kind of a nerd—smart but totally out of it socially. And Greg wouldn't ever let up on him. He was always needling poor Hugh, taunting him and embarrassing him dreadfully in front of other people. Erin was certain that Greg's tormenting and his belittling comments had finally pushed Hugh over the edge. And the worst of it was that Greg felt no remorse. He'd even joked about it, telling Erin that this proved Hugh couldn't do anything right, even commit suicide.

Now she sighed, realizing all over again that there was no way she could have kept on with Greg. Once she'd started to see his real character under all that glamour and charm, she didn't feel the same way about him. And she would have hated herself if she'd ignored his cruelty to others, just so she'd still be going with the boy everyone else wanted.

Only Becky knew about Erin's suspicions, and she agreed that Greg could have been partly responsible for Hugh's attempted suicide, even though it wasn't something they could prove. And of course Greg knew what Erin thought. He'd been really angry when she'd accused him of driving Hugh over the edge, and even angrier when she said she didn't want to go out with him anymore.

Suddenly Erin wondered what Greg would do once he realized she was serious about breaking up with him. He was used to getting his own way and wasn't likely to accept Erin's decision without some kind of retaliation. I'll bet he starts bad-mouthing me before long, Erin said to herself.

Then another thought popped into her mind. Could it be Greg making those creepy hang-up calls she'd been getting here at Abby's house? He knew she usually sat for Abby in the afternoons and now he knew that she'd be there all week. Erin ran her fingers through her hair, pushing it back from her face. I don't want to believe it, she thought, but I wouldn't be surprised.

CHAPTER THREE

Abby had just finished placing the salt and pepper shakers in the exact center of the dinner table when the phone rang. "Let me get it," she said, and hurried to the small desk where the phone sat.

"Hello," Abby said in her most grown-up voice. After a moment Erin heard her say uncertainly, "Who is this?" Oh, no, Erin thought. It's that jerk again, and this time he's breathing in Abby's ear. That's just too much.

Already rehearsing the blistering words she planned to use, Erin quickly dried her hands and crossed the room. Holding out her hand to take the phone, she saw Abby's look of confusion. The child's face was puckered up as if she were about to burst into tears. It was the last straw. "Hello. Who is this?" Erin barked into the phone.

There was a brief silence and then she heard a woman's voice. "Who is this?"

Feeling a little foolish, Erin said in a calmer tone, "This is the Peters residence. Can I help you?"

The woman on the other end said, "I need to talk to John." She sounded a little upset.

Erin replied, "I'm sorry, but Mr. Peters isn't here right now. Can I take a message?"

"Well, I have to talk to him. It's terribly important. He has to be there. Tell him to answer the phone. He's just avoiding me and I've got to talk to him."

Erin wasn't quite sure what to say. She answered slowly, "Really, Mr. Peters isn't home. Won't you give me your name?"

With astonishment she heard the woman say, "This is his wife."

Before the woman could go on, Erin said, "Mrs. Peters? Oh, hi. This is Erin Moore." Surely Mrs. Peters would remember her. She'd baby-sat a number of times for Abby when she was really little, before her mother had gone away.

But Annette Peters said only, "Erin? Oh. Well, I have to speak to John. I've got to make my plans. After all, places get booked up so early these days, and I have to find a nice place to take my baby. I'm going to go away with her this summer—just me and my baby, all alone. So I have to talk to him. Just go and get him.''

"Well," Erin began. She didn't know quite what to make of the whole thing. "I'm sorry, Mrs. Peters, he really isn't here. He's out of town on a business trip and I'm here taking care of Abby. Mr. Peters won't be back until the end of the week, but I'll be sure to tell him that you called. Let me write down your number."

Annette Peters recited her phone number calmly while Erin wrote it down. But then her voice rose again shrilly. "You tell him that I need to speak to him and that it's important!"

"Okay, Mrs. Peters, I will," Erin responded before she realized she was talking to a dead line. Annette had already hung up.

As Erin put the receiver down, Abby said in a small voice, "That was my mommy."

"Yes, honey, it was." Erin didn't know what else to say.

"Can we have a story now?" Abby asked.

Erin looked at the child. "Sure, honey. Just let me put the macaroni in the oven and you go pick out a book."

When they sat down on the couch, Abby snuggled close to Erin, one small hand holding Erin's arm while the other clutched her teddy bear to her side. When the story was over, she ate her dinner quietly and then went upstairs for her bath. As Erin helped her into the tub and left her to play with her boats for a while, she realized that the child hadn't mentioned her mother's phone call again all evening.

In Abby's room Erin got out the child's nightie and turned down the bed. As she picked up the scattered books and replaced them in the bookshelves, she thought about Annette's call. It had been a complete surprise. After Annette had left a year and a half ago, no one Erin knew had seen her or heard from her. In fact, now that she thought about it, neither Abby nor Mr. Peters ever mentioned the child's mother.

Erin didn't know what had happened. After a while it was almost as if Mrs. Peters had died. How amazing that she'd suddenly reappeared and was planning to go on a vacation with Abby. She'd certainly sounded upset, though. And the way she kept insisting that Mr. Peters was avoiding her phone calls made Erin think that there must be some problem that hadn't been worked out. Erin wished she knew more about the situation. For instance, why wasn't Abby spending this week with her mother, instead of staying at her dad's house with a baby-sitter?

Absent mindedly Erin pushed her hair back

behind her ears. What if Abby asked her about this trip with her mother? I won't bring it up unless Abby does, Erin decided. But I wish I understood what's going on.

As Erin went into the bathroom to hand Abby her towel and to make sure she brushed her teeth, she felt a pang of sympathy for her. After the last story of the evening, Erin gave the little girl an extra hug and kiss and tucked her into bed with her bear. "Good-night, honey, sleep tight."

Downstairs, Erin made herself a cup of coffee and then picked up the book she'd been trying to read. I just can't deal with any more of the causes of World War I tonight, she decided. Why did I pick such a boring topic for my paper? Instead she flipped through the TV listings and saw that *Casablanca* was on cable. Well, it's the wrong war, Erin thought, laughing to herself. But it's such a great movie.

An hour later Erin was completely caught up in Ingrid Bergman's desperate efforts to get travel papers for her resistance-hero husband. Even though she knew how it ended, this wartime tale of love and sacrifice never failed to move her. She sat forward on the couch as the band struck up the "Marseillaise"; despite the presence of the German officers, the motley crowd at Rick's bar gathered their courage and one by one stood to attention. By the end of the song they were all singing, and Erin felt a lump in her throat.

When the movie was over, Erin went up to get ready for bed. She didn't consider herself any nosier than the next person, but she couldn't help wondering about Annette Peters. Her mother had always said Mrs. Peters was "so high-strung" and Erin had to agree that Annette had a kind of thoroughbred elegance, full of nervous energy. Tall and almost painfully thin, Annette might have been a model. Lucky Abby had inherited her mother's naturally curly blond hair and big gray eyes. She'll be as pretty as Annette when she grows up, Erin thought.

For a moment she let herself wish that she had those looks. Then she laughed at herself. Not in my family, she thought.

It was funny to see how heredity worked. Sean looks like Dad, but I look just like Mom, Erin reflected. We have the same thick straight black hair and fair skin, and our eyes are the same shade of blue. And Mom is still really pretty, so I guess it could be worse, she thought sleepily as she climbed into bed and turned out the light.

The shrill sound of screaming woke her and Erin swam up out of a confused dream. She sat up, her heart pounding, and looked at the clock, but it wasn't where it was supposed to be. It had moved to the other side of the bed—the green digital numbers read 2:04, and then she came fully awake. She wasn't at home in her own bed. She was in the guest room of the Peters house, and Abby was screaming in terror.

Flinging back the covers, Erin raced to the child's room. "Abby, what's wrong? What's the matter, honey?"

The little girl was huddled in a ball at the foot of her bed, the blanket twisted half onto the floor. Erin reached out and touched her shoulder, and Abby flinched away. "Mommy, don't be mad at me!" she whimpered piteously.

Erin said softly, "Abby, come on, wake up. You're having a bad dream." The girl's eyes opened and she gazed blankly at Erin. "Come on," Erin urged gently, "let's get you straightened out." She shifted the small body toward the head of the bed and pulled up the covers. Then she picked up Abby's teddy bear from the floor and tucked him in beside her.

Abby sighed and turned over. Erin sat on the edge of the bed and carefully smoothed the damp curls away from Abby's forehead. The child seemed sound asleep again, and after a moment Erin tiptoed out of the room.

Back in bed, she lay wondering if there was something more she should have done for Abby.

But as she thought drowsily that she'd get up and check on the little girl in a few minutes, she drifted once more into sleep.

Just before dawn she woke again. Gray light seeped in around the curtains as she sat up. Was Abby calling her? Then she heard the scared little voice. "Mommy, don't! Please don't!"

Erin ran to the child's room. She sat down on the bed and, gathering Abby into her arms, she rocked the little girl against her body. "It's all right, Abby, I'm here," she crooned softly.

Abby muttered some disconnected words. Erin bent to hear her, but she couldn't make any sense of what the child was saying. Leaning back against the pillow, she held Abby close. "Go to sleep, honey, you just had a bad dream," she repeated. The little girl shifted restlessly and wrapped one small arm around Erin's neck. As Erin slid down to a more comfortable position, she thought helplessly, What should I do?

Erin opened her eyes to dazzling morning sunlight and saw Abby staring at her in amazement. "You slept in my bed with me," the little girl said in a puzzled voice.

"Yes. You had a bad dream last night," Erin explained cautiously.

"I did? I don't remember. Is it time to get up yet? I'm hungry."

Erin laughed. "I suppose it's time. What would you like for breakfast?"

"Pancakes?" Abby asked hopefully.

"Why not?"

"Goody!" Abby scrambled off the bed and went into the bathroom, but when Erin began to get up, she found she was stiff and sore from sharing the small bed. I hope I don't have to do that again, she thought. But was it possible that the little girl had forgotten all about those terrifying dreams?

Just as the two of them were finishing their breakfast, the doorbell rang. Walking to the door, Erin was amazed to see her parents standing on the porch. When she opened the door, she saw that her mother's face looked pale and drawn. "Mom, what's the matter?"

"Oh, Erin, the most terrible thing! Sean's had an accident." Erin gasped but her mother went on, "He fell on the ski slope—I knew it was too dangerous. And now they have to take him to the hospital in Quebec. They said it was his leg and they wouldn't let me talk to him."

"Oh, Mom, how awful," Erin said.

"I never should have let him go on this trip. I just knew . . ." Erin's mother gulped and then went on, "We're on our way to the airport right now. But, honey, I hate to leave you all on your own. Will you be all right?"

"Of course I will, Mom. Don't worry."

Erin's father put his arm around her mother's shoulders. "We're both pretty upset," he said. "I know you'll be okay, and we'll call you from Quebec as soon as we find out how Sean's doing. And don't forget, if you need anything, you can always call your Aunt Noreen." He paused and then said, "I'm sure it's nothing too serious, Erin. Don't worry."

Her dad's voice sounded strained and Erin heard his uncertainty and concern. "I'm sure he's going to be fine, Dad. Thanks for letting me know. Give Sean my love and don't worry about me."

Giving each of them a hug, Erin watched as they walked to their car and drove away. Then she got Abby settled in the dining room with her Lego set. "I'm going upstairs to take a shower, honey," she said. "I'll be down in a few minutes."

While the warm spray beat the remaining stiffness out of her muscles, Erin thought about her brother. From what her mom had said, it sounded like he'd broken his leg. He'd probably come home with a huge cast. Poor Sean, he'd been looking forward to this trip so much. I'll bet he's furious that this happened on the second day he was there, Erin thought as she rinsed the shampoo out of her hair.

Pulling on jeans and a sweatshirt, she shook out her mane of shoulder-length dark hair and tied it back with a yellow ribbon that matched her shirt. Erin grinned wryly at herself in the mirror. Did Daddy really think I would call Aunt Noreen—my least favorite relative? She always makes me feel totally incompetent, as if I can't do anything right. She's the last person I'd want to talk to if I was worried about something.

As she walked down the stairs, Erin noticed how quiet the house was. For the first time she felt alone and a little lonely, knowing that her parents were gone and she was now completely in charge. She shivered; she didn't hear a sound. A sudden stab of fear went through her. Was Abby all right?

She hurried the rest of the way downstairs and rushed into the dining room. Abby looked up from her Lego construction. "Look, I built a house. It's got windows and everything. But I need you to help me make the roof," the little girl told her.

Feeling absurdly relieved, Erin knelt down and together they carefully attached the small red and white pieces that formed the roof. When they were finished they both sat back and admired it. Then the phone rang and Abby ran to answer it. Erin saw the child's face light up as she said, "Hi, Dad. Guess what? Me and Erin had pancakes for breakfast!" She talked for a few moments more and then handed the phone to Erin.

"Hi, Mr. Peters."

Through a rather crackly connection she could hear him say, "Hello, Erin. I wanted to let you know that I won't be in the hotel for the next couple of days. They need me to go look at some building sites and I'll be roughing it. I probably won't be anywhere near a phone. So I thought I'd check in and make sure you're both all right before I left."

Bored with Erin's half of the conversation, Abby went to the back door. She motioned toward the outside, and when Erin opened the back door for her, she tiptoed outside and closed it quietly behind her. Through the kitchen window Erin could see her stealthily trying to creep up on the cat from next door.

Taking the opportunity to speak freely with Abby out of the room, Erin said into the phone, "Well, everything really is okay, but I wanted to ask you, does Abby have nightmares very often?"

"No. Why?" Mr. Peters sounded surprised.

"Oh, last night she woke up twice and she was obviously having bad dreams. So I wondered—"

Mr. Peters cut in abruptly. "What were the dreams about?"

"I don't know exactly," Erin said slowly. "She said, 'Mommy, don't be mad at me.' But I told her it was just a dream. I stayed with her the rest of the night and she seems fine this morning. She doesn't remember any of it."

Erin heard Mr. Peters say, "Damn!" Then he spoke into the phone. "I can't imagine what brought that on."

"I don't know," Erin said. "But the other thing I wanted to tell you is that your wife called last night."

"Annette called?" Mr. Peters sounded surprised. "What did she say?"

"Well, Abby talked to her first, and then when I got on the phone, she seemed kind of upset that you weren't here. She wanted to talk to you about the vacation she's taking Abby on this summer." When Mr. Peters didn't say anything, she added, "I said you wouldn't be back until the end of the week."

"Okay." His voice was angry. "I told her not to call the house. I don't want her to upset Abby. But I'll get in touch with her as soon as I can. In the meantime, if Annette should call again, I don't want Abby to speak to her."

"Okay," Erin said dubiously.

Mr. Peters's voice was fading in and out as

the connection got worse. "Annette is not to see Abby or talk to her under any circumstances. Do you understand?"

"Yes, Mr. Peters."

"This connection is terrible; I'll have to hang up," he said. "I know you're taking good care of Abby—I'll talk to both of you soon."

Erin hung up the phone feeling bewildered. She was shaken by the conversation she'd had with Mr. Peters. It seemed so strange; Annette was the little girl's mother, after all. Why wasn't she allowed to see Abby?

CHAPTER FOUR

Pushing her hair behind her ears, Erin went outside. It was another beautiful day, and soon she and Abby were on their way to the park a few blocks away.

When they got there, Abby raced off to the slide. Erin sat down on the edge of the sandbox, pushing up her sleeves to catch the warm sunshine on her bare arms. Then she felt someone standing behind her. "Oh, hi, Erin."

Turning, Erin smiled. "Hi, Jill. What are you doing here?" Somehow Jill Saunders wasn't the type to spend her Sunday afternoon in the park with a bunch of little kids. Automatically looking around for Jill's boyfriend, Erin asked, "Where's Bruce?"

"Can you believe it, he had to go out with his folks and visit his grandmother in the nursing home today. I probably won't even see him until tomorrow,'' Jill said with a theatrical sigh. "So my mom decided that it was the perfect time for me to take my little brother and his friend to the park, and here I am.'' Gesturing toward the two little boys by the swings, Jill suddenly yelled, "Timmy, don't throw sand!"

The two boys looked at Jill and then got on the swings. Jill sighed. "Don't you just want to wring their necks sometimes?'' she said to Erin. Then she sat down beside her.

"How was the party last night?'' Erin asked.

"Oh, it was okay,'' Jill replied. "But actually Bruce and I left kind of early. Everybody was drinking a lot and some of the guys were throwing up in the bushes. To be honest, I didn't want to be there when Jimmy's parents got home.''

"Sounds great!'' Erin grinned at her friend.

Jill smiled, too. "Yeah, that kind of thing gets old pretty fast.'' Then she said more seriously, "Listen, Erin, I hate to be the one to tell you this, but Greg was there with Debbie Williams. She was really all over him; you know how she is.'' Jill wrinkled her nose in distaste. Then she added, "It didn't look to me as if he was having such a great time, though. I think you could get him back if you put a little effort into it.'' She looked at Erin questioningly.

"But I don't want to get him back," Erin said coolly.

"Why not?"

Erin waved her hand dismissively. "Oh, you know how it is."

When she didn't go on, Jill said, "Well, I'm sorry about it—I liked the four of us doing stuff together."

"Me, too," Erin said, "but some things just aren't meant to be, I guess."

Before long Abby was ready to go home. As they walked along, Erin wished again that Becky hadn't gone away. There was no way to explain to Jill why she'd broken up with Greg. It would just sound like sour grapes and it wouldn't do anyone any good. Besides, Jill and Bruce were no doubt still going to see a lot of Greg. With a pang of loneliness, Erin realized that she really would miss the good times the four of them had had.

As they turned into the path that led up to the front steps, Erin reached in her pocket for the key. Glancing up at the house, she froze in horror. What was that shadow that had moved across the living room window? Someone was inside the house!

Grabbing Abby's arm, Erin said quickly, "Wait a minute, honey." Her mind was racing as she tried to decide what to do. Was it a burglar? She couldn't help remembering the phone calls—had they really been made by someone who was waiting for the house to be empty?

Erin tried to convince herself that she was imagining things. But she didn't really think so. The shadow inside the house had been real— she was sure she'd seen someone moving around in there. And one thing was certain—she wasn't going to take Abby into that house until she knew it was safe.

Still clutching Abby's arm, Erin tried to think what to do. She looked along the street, hoping to see some solid citizen who could be trusted to help, but no one was out on this balmy spring day. Across the street, however, she saw that the Jensens' car was in the driveway.

Keeping her voice calm and even, Erin said to Abby, "I just remembered something I need to ask Mrs. Jensen. Come on, let's go across the street and see if she's home." I'll ask if I can use the phone, she thought, and I'll call the police. I just hope I can do it without upsetting Abby.

When Erin rang the doorbell, Mrs. Jensen appeared and was delighted to see them. "Hi, Abby, I haven't seen you in a while. Come on in and I'll see if I can find a little something for you to nibble on."

The Jensens' big black Labrador, Thor, appeared and Abby gave him a hug while Erin explained, "I need to use your phone, Mrs. Jensen."

"Oh, sure, just let me get Abby settled—I have some fresh peanut butter cookies I just made yesterday. But is anything wrong? You look a little upset."

Moving out of Abby's earshot, Erin confessed, "Well, yes, I am upset. You'll think this sounds crazy but I'm sure I saw someone inside the house and I'm afraid to go in. I want to call the police."

"Goodness, that's terrible, of course you're upset. Let me just get Henry up here—he'll know what to do." Mrs. Jensen opened the door to the basement and called, "Henry? Henry! Come up here a minute."

When Mr. Jensen appeared, he looked even older and more fragile than his wife. But when he'd heard Erin's story, he said briskly, "Well, I'll just take Thor over and have a good look around. If anyone is there, Thor will let me know."

"Well," Erin said doubtfully, "if you're sure it will be—"

"It will be my pleasure," he assured her formally. Soon he had put on Thor's leash, and Erin was crossing the street with him to the

Peters house. She opened the door and they both went inside with the big black dog.

They searched the ground floor of the house without finding anyone. As they did, Mr. Jensen spoke to Thor in a loud voice. "Good boy, Thor. Can you find anyone? Good work, boy." Then he informed Erin that they would search the basement next. "We want to scare him if he's here," he told her. "And if he got in through the basement, he can get out that way before we get down there. If he's upstairs, this will give him a chance to get out. There's no point in taking unnecessary risks," he concluded seriously.

But there was no one in the basement, and they heard no sound of escaping footsteps from upstairs. Mr. Jensen and Thor went carefully through the upstairs bedrooms and the bathroom, and when they had finished it was obvious to Erin that there was no one hiding in the house.

"I'm so glad you were home," she told him gratefully. "Thanks so much for doing this. I feel really dumb—"

Mr. Jensen held up his hand. "Not at all, my dear," he said. "Better safe than sorry, and Thor and I were glad to be of service."

Returning with him to collect Abby, Erin's legs were trembling with the release of tension.

I must be going crazy or something, she thought, seeing ghosts and burglars every time I turn around.

But as she and Abby crossed the street once more, Erin felt a strong reluctance to enter the house again. What could possibly happen next?

That evening, after Abby was in bed, Erin sat in Mr. Peters's den making out a shopping list for the next day. She'd always liked this room with its book-lined walls and beautiful fireplace.

The silver picture frame on a low shelf caught her attention. Why was it empty? She stood up to take a closer look and for a moment wondered, could Mr. Peters have taken the photo of himself and Abby with him on his trip? Then she thought, of course not. Abby copied that picture in her drawing yesterday morning. And I distinctly remember putting it back after she'd finished.

Maybe somehow the photo had slipped down out of the frame. But when she walked over and picked it up, the photograph was nowhere to be seen. Erin stood there staring through the clear glass at the blank cardboard backing. A shiver ran through her body. What had happened to the photograph?

She returned the frame to the shelf and stepped back. Then she noticed the scrap of paper on the floor in front of the bookcase. Bending to retrieve it, Erin saw that it was a small piece of the missing photograph. She turned slowly, her eyes searching the floor, but no more scraps were visible.

Unwillingly she moved to the large wastebasket by the desk, and the tiny hairs on the back of her neck rose as she saw the rest of the pieces in a small heap at the bottom. Someone had maliciously ripped Mr. Peters's treasured photo to shreds.

Erin stood transfixed in horror. She'd been right after all! Somebody *had* been in the house— somebody had been in that very room, carefully removing the picture of Abby and Mr. Peters and then systematically destroying it.

Her mind raced. Who could it have been? Why would anyone do such a thing? She couldn't think of any rational reason. And the weirdest part of it was that nothing else in the house had been disturbed. She sank into the desk chair, trembling as a wave of fear washed over her. What was going on?

Her thoughts in confusion, Erin sat at the desk and looked blankly at the scrap of photo still in her hand. The big old house was silent and still. Earlier Erin had found the silence restful, but now it seemed almost threatening.

Suddenly she heard a click and then a scraping noise coming from the kitchen. It was the unmistakable sound of a key being turned in the back door! Erin froze and her heart seemed to leap into her throat. Someone was coming inside!

CHAPTER FIVE

Her pulse pounding, Erin desperately tried to think. If she called the police from the phone at the desk, the intruder would surely hear her. But there was another phone upstairs in the master bedroom. Could she creep quietly to the stairs and get up them without being seen? For a brief moment she thought of trying to escape through the front door, but she couldn't leave Abby alone in the house. Even as these possibilities tumbled through her brain, Erin wondered if this was the same person who'd been in the house earlier and had torn up the photograph.

Erin heard the heavy tread of footsteps on the kitchen floor. Whoever it was, he certainly wasn't trying to hide his presence. Did he think there was no one in the house? Quickly Erin made up her mind. She'd sneak upstairs and call the police from there, hoping that whatever the intruder wanted was on the first floor. Arming herself with the poker from the fireplace, she moved stealthily out of the den and made her way soundlessly through the living room to the front hall.

She had put her foot on the bottom step when a voice stopped her. "Hey! Wait a minute. What are you doing here?"

Erin whirled around to face the young man who stood in the kitchen doorway, an expression of amazement on his face. He didn't look much older than Erin herself and he certainly didn't appear to be dangerous. As the thumping of her heart began to subside, she realized that she knew him. He was Dan Peters, Abby's half-brother.

Feeling a little foolish, Erin said, "Oh, hi, Dan. It's me, Erin Moore. I'm here staying with Abby." Then with more assurance she asked, "What are you doing here?"

Dan still looked puzzled but then his face cleared. "Oh, right. I forgot. It's this week that Dad's away. I thought he'd be here. I hope I didn't scare you, coming in unannounced like that."

"Well, you did. A bit," Erin said lightly as she edged back across the living room trying to return the poker as unobtrusively as possible. But her attempt at nonchalance didn't fool Dan.

"Right," he said with a grin. "You always walk around with a poker in your hand." Then he added more seriously, "I really am sorry. I didn't know you were here."

"That's okay," Erin told him. After a pause, she said, "I was just about to make some coffee. Would you like some?"

"Sure." Dan followed her into the kitchen. "I just stopped by to pick up some camping gear," he explained as Erin put the water on to boil. "I had it all planned to go skiing over spring break, but that fell through, so I'm going to go up to our cabin in the Berkshires for the rest of the week." Erin nodded and Dan went on, "I guess I'll go collect my stuff—it's all down in the basement, or at least I hope that's where I left it."

He clumped down the stairs as Erin measured coffee into the filter. Her hands shook and she realized how frightened she had been. Thank goodness it turned out to be Dan, she thought in relief. At least he's part of the family and has a perfect right to walk into the house. Erin didn't know Dan very well, but she'd seen him around lots of times when he was home on vacations from his prep school. Now he was in his first year at Amherst. Erin couldn't remember all the details but she had heard that Dan's mother—Mr. Peters's first wife—had died when Dan was very young.

When they were both sitting at the kitchen table with their coffee and some of Mrs. Jensen's peanut butter cookies, Erin couldn't think of anything to say. Dan was so good-looking and self-assured, and somehow she felt shy and awkward around him. But he didn't appear to notice. "Good cookies," he said as he reached for another. "Did you make them?"

"No, I can't take credit for these," Erin told him. "Mrs. Jensen across the street gave them to us."

Dan grinned. "I should have known," he said. "She was always trying to fatten me up when I was a kid and I was always happy to let her do it." He sipped his coffee, and then went on, "Aren't you finishing high school this spring?" When Erin nodded, he asked, "Where are you going to college?"

"Holyoke."

"Great. I'll probably see you then. Got any idea of what you want to major in yet?"

"Depends which week you ask me." Erin laughed. "But tell me about Amherst. They have a combined program with Holyoke and a couple of other schools, don't they? How does that work?"

Dan launched into a glowing description of the classes and professors. He made it all sound so exciting that Erin felt as if she could hardly wait for next September when she'd be at school there, too.

At last he paused for breath. "I can't think of what else to tell you," he said. "But I know you'll love it."

"It sounds terrific," Erin told him. "Amherst should hire you to recruit students." A slight sound caught her ear. "I think I hear Abby—I'll just go up and check on her," she said as she stood up and moved toward the stairs.

But when Erin tiptoed into the little girl's room, Abby was sleeping peacefully, one arm flopped across her teddy bear. Erin pulled up the covers around her shoulders and then went back down the stairs.

"Everything okay?" Dan asked as she came into the kitchen.

"She's fine," Erin said. "But she's been having nightmares, so I wanted to make sure she's all right." She shook her head. "Whatever I heard may not even have been Abby. I guess I'm a little jumpy—some weird things have been happening."

"What kind of weird things?" Dan's voice sounded genuinely interested, and Erin found herself recounting the unsettling incidents that had occurred since she came to stay with Abby—the phone caller who listened without saying anything, Erin's certainty that she'd seen someone inside the house, and her discovery of the torn-up photograph. Her voice shook as she told him this last part and she was afraid she sounded silly to have been so scared. But it was such a relief to pour it all out to someone else.

When she stopped talking, Dan said, "No wonder you were so spooked when I came waltzing through the door after dark. But you know, Erin, I can think of perfectly ordinary explanations for everything that's happened. Those phone calls—people get them all the time. I'm sure some idiot was trying to call Joe's Pizzeria and didn't have the courtesy to tell you he'd dialed wrong. And as for someone being inside the house today, maybe there was and maybe there wasn't, but you certainly handled it okay." He smiled at her reassuringly. "I mean, I can see that it was scary, but nothing really happened."

Dan stood up and went over to the stove as Erin said slowly, "You might be right. But that doesn't explain about the photograph. Somebody had to be in this house to tear it up." Just thinking about it gave Erin the creeps and she shivered in spite of herself. Dan leaned over the table to pour coffee into their cups and she was aware of his strong lean body close to hers.

He didn't reply until he was sitting across the table from her again. "It must have been Abby," he said then. "She's probably upset that Dad's away and she tore up the picture because she was mad at him. But then she didn't want to admit it to you."

"Well," Erin said doubtfully, "I suppose it's possible."

"Of course it is. Who else could it have been?"

"Oh, I don't know." Erin pushed her hair away from her face. "I guess I get worried because I feel so responsible for her, with your dad so far away. And then these nightmares. I forgot to tell you that her mother had called and Abby seemed upset when she talked to her, and it was that night that she had the bad dreams. She sounded terrified and she was saying something about her mother. I didn't know what to do to help her."

Dan looked at her and then reached over to touch her arm. "Hey, don't get so upset. They were only dreams," he said gently.

Erin shrugged helplessly. "I know. But why would your dad tell me that Abby isn't supposed to see Annette or even talk to her?"

"I don't know." Dan paused for a moment,

frowning slightly. "Actually I never knew Annette very well at all. When she and my dad got married, I was going through a rough time and Dad sent me off to boarding school. I only saw her on vacations and even then I was busy with camp and stuff like that. So—I know she has problems, but I'm not sure exactly what they are. She left Dad with a little kid to take care of, though, and maybe they're still going through some kind of fight about that." He glanced at his watch. "Hey, it's getting late—I'd better hit the road."

Erin watched as Dan collected his various pieces of camping gear. "Thanks for the coffee," he told her, hoisting the backpack to his shoulder. "It was good to see you. And next time I'll try to let you know I'm coming." He grinned and Erin smiled back at him.

"Good," she replied. "And thanks for listening—I feel a lot better about things."

At the door Dan turned to look at her, his dark eyes serious. "You know, the one who got the worst of things when my dad and Annette split up was probably Abby. She's been through a lot for a little kid—maybe it's not surprising if she has nightmares now and then." Then he smiled warmly at her. "So long, Erin. I hope nothing more happens to disturb your dreams."

He let himself out and the door shut firmly behind him.

Erin rinsed the coffee cups and stuck them in the dishwasher. She was yawning, and she knew Abby would wake up early. As she went around the downstairs turning off lights and making a final check of the door and window locks, Erin realized how much more relaxed she felt after talking to Dan. He had made her feel that these unsettling episodes could have happened to anybody. It was just a run of bad luck, she told herself firmly.

The wind was rising, and by the time Erin got upstairs she could hear the old windows rattling in their frames. She looked in on Abby, who was still fast asleep. As she stood brushing her teeth, the small bathroom window was illuminated by a flash of lightning and then she heard an explosive clap of thunder. Moments later the first heavy drops of rain tapped sharply on the roof.

She lowered her bedroom window until it was only open a crack, then made sure the flashlight was in the drawer of the nightstand beside the bed. Power failures were all too common in Wentworth during thunderstorms and she didn't want to have to feel her way into Abby's room in total darkness.

Then Erin turned off the lights in the room

and stood at the window, looking out at the pelting rain. Another bolt of lightning slashed across the sky. Erin shivered, hugging herself as a fine spray of wind-swept water whooshed against the glass. Too bad we didn't know this was coming, she thought. Dan could have spent the night here and not gotten caught in this deluge. But really, she admitted to herself, what I mean is, it would have been nice not to be alone on a night like this.

Erin got into bed and pulled the blankets up to her chin. Though she had felt sleepy earlier, she now found herself wide awake, her eyes refusing to close. She couldn't stop thinking about her conversation with Dan. If only she could believe Abby had torn up that photograph. Everything else he'd said made sense, but Erin couldn't imagine the little girl doing such a thing.

She turned onto her side, punching her pillow into a more comfortable position. It was all so confusing. She squirmed about in the bed again and then tried lying very still, hoping that the steady beat of rain against the window would lull her to sleep. But instead a new and more alarming thought leapt into her mind. What if Dan himself had come to the house that morning and destroyed the photo of his dad and Abby?

She told herself not to be ridiculous, but once planted, the idea wouldn't go away. Dan certainly had a key to the house and, of course, he could come in any time he wanted to. After all, he lived there. If he somehow felt that Abby had come between his dad and himself, then destroying that particular photograph made a certain sick sense.

Erin really didn't know much about Dan except what he had told her that evening. How could she be sure he was actually on his way to the Berkshires? What was to stop him from coming back to the house and doing something else? Maybe he wouldn't be satisfied with just damaging a picture of Abby. He might try to hurt the child herself. Could Abby be in danger from her own half-brother?

Erin sat bolt upright in bed. Of course! It must have been Dan who'd made all those phone calls. He was trying to find a time when the house was empty so he could come in and start on his secret reign of terror.

Hold on a minute, Erin told herself. You're letting your imagination run away with you again. It's really time to get some sleep. She snuggled back down under the covers and glanced at the illuminated numbers of the digital clock beside the bed. Just as she registered that it was 1:14 in the morning, the lighted numbers disappeared. The power was out.

Oh, no, she thought tiredly. Just what I need. She fumbled for the flashlight and climbed out of bed. The floor felt chilly under her feet as she made her way to the telephone in the master bedroom. Probably everyone in the world was calling the power company, but she'd add her complaint to their list.

As she reached the doorway, the phone began to ring, making her jump. Whoever was calling at this hour must have an urgent reason. Could it be Mr. Peters? Or what if something was wrong with Sean and her own parents were trying to reach Erin?

She grabbed the receiver. "Hello?" she said breathlessly.

When no one replied, she tried again. "Hello? Hello, who is it?" But still there was no answer, although she could hear that the line was open.

Trembling, Erin replaced the receiver slowly. She felt close to tears as she returned to her room. It hadn't been a family emergency—it had been the anonymous caller.

The loud ring of the phone in the middle of the night had been frightening enough, but the really terrifying part was the feeling that someone was secretly watching her. Had he waited for the power to go off in the house before calling and scaring her half to death? Was that what he wanted? she wondered hopelessly.

Back in bed Erin lay rigid, afraid to go to sleep now in case the phone rang again. It was so frustrating to know that there was nothing at all she could do to stop these calls.

Her earlier suspicions of Dan seemed foolish to her now. He had absolutely no reason to torment her. But Greg did.

Erin felt a chill creep up her spine. Could Greg really be the person making the phone calls? Did he want to harass her and terrify her while she was here all alone? He knew that she was staying at the Peters house, taking care of Abby, and she could imagine him gloating at the sound of her anger and helpless fear.

Erin felt sure she was right. First thing in the morning she'd call Greg and tell him what she thought of him. He wasn't going to drive her crazy, no matter how hard he tried.

CHAPTER SIX

As Abby was getting ready for school the next morning, the phone rang. Erin's heart was pounding as she picked it up. If it was Greg, she was going to be ready. "Hello? Peters residence."

A woman's voice said, "I want to talk to my baby. Put her on the phone."

It sounded like Annette, but Erin asked, "Who is this? Is this Mrs. Peters?"

"Yes, it is," the impatient voice replied. "I want to speak to my baby."

"Well, uh—" Erin wasn't sure what to say. It seemed so cruel not to let Annette talk to her own daughter, but Mr. Peters had been very firm. He'd said she wasn't to see or talk to Abby under any circumstances. Erin tried to think of a polite way to handle the situation.

Finally she said, "I'm afraid she can't talk right now, Mrs. Peters."

"Don't lie to me—I know she's there," the woman said angrily. "Let me speak to her immediately."

"I can't," Erin told her, feeling even more awkward about the whole thing. "I'm sorry."

"Now listen. I don't know who you are, but you've got no right to keep my baby from me. I'm her mother. They're always trying to take her away from me, and I can't stand it anymore."

What can I say to her? Erin wondered desperately. She sounds totally out of control. And what does she mean, she doesn't know who I am? Trying to sound calm, she said, "This is Erin Moore, Mrs. Peters. I told you before that I'm staying here with Abby. I'm really sorry, but Mr. Peters said you weren't supposed to talk to Abby. I'll be happy to—"

Cutting her off, Annette shouted, "He can't do that to me! Put him on the phone this instant, I'll tell him who's supposed to do what. I should have known, they're all against me—" Her voice broke in what sounded like a sob. Then she went on disjointedly, "No matter how hard I try, nothing goes the way I want it to. All I wanted was my baby. I have to tell him—" Her voice rose again as she demanded, "Put that cruel devil on the phone. He's afraid to talk to me, isn't he? But I know my rights! I want to talk to him right now!''

Abby was standing in the kitchen doorway, watching Erin with a puzzled expression. Erin's hands were trembling, but she gave the child a reassuring smile and then spoke into the phone as firmly as she could. "He's not here, and he won't be back until the end of the week. I think you should call him then and get everything straightened out." Without waiting to hear any more, she hung up.

"Who was that?" Abby asked.

"Someone who wanted to talk to your dad," Erin told her. "Come on, let's get you to school."

Abby skipped along cheerfully as they walked the few blocks to her nursery school, but for Erin the morning was spoiled. She couldn't get the conversation with Annette out of her head, and as she detoured to the grocery store after dropping Abby off, she kept wondering if there was some way she could have handled it better. She felt a little spurt of anger at Mr. Peters. He'd left her in a very difficult position—he shouldn't expect her to be the go-between in this quarrel with his ex-wife.

Erin walked back from the store with her bag of groceries. She hoped she'd remembered everything—she wasn't used to shopping for a household. In a way it was kind of fun to be in charge of a house and to make all the decisions about meals and things like that. But as she unlocked the front door of the Peters house, she realized that in other ways this job had turned out to be more than she'd bargained for.

In the kitchen Erin glanced warily at the phone before starting to put away the food she'd bought. What was she going to say if Annette called again? The whole situation was so confusing, and Erin felt torn. She wasn't sure where her loyalties lay. Of course, Mr. Peters trusted her to do her job the way he wanted it done, and that seemed to include keeping Annette from contact with Abby. He'd always been nice to her in his somewhat distant way, and Erin couldn't betray the confidence he'd shown in her.

On the other hand, Erin was feeling kind of sorry for Annette. It must be awful for her to be kept away from her own daughter. No wonder she'd been almost hysterical on the phone this morning.

Still, it was a little strange that Annette hadn't known who Erin was. When she had been living in this house, Annette had seemed to really like Erin. She was always asking about how school was going and they'd had some long conversations about movies they'd both enjoyed.

The more she thought about it, the more peculiar it was.

She must have changed somehow, Erin thought, or something must have happened that I don't know about. It seemed that one day they were all here together and the next day she was gone and nobody saw her after that. Unwillingly Erin found herself wondering whether Annette's disappearance had something to do with Abby. She'd tried to believe that the child's piteous cries were only a nightmare. But what if the little girl was really afraid of her mother?

Erin sighed. With Becky unavailable, she couldn't think of anyone else to discuss it with. Of course many of her other friends from school, like Jill, had stayed home for spring break. But as she ran through their names in her mind, Erin knew she wouldn't feel comfortable talking about the Peters family with any of them. She never discussed secrets with anyone but Becky. Or if her parents were home, she could talk to her mom.

Of course, her dad had suggested that she call her Aunt Noreen if she had any problems. Fat chance, Erin thought. I know just how it would go. Aunt Noreen will make it crystal clear that she was right all along—I'm too immature and unable to handle responsibility. And at the same time she'll tell me that I'm being ridiculous to worry and that she can't see what the problem is. Then she'll offer to drive in and help me out and won't take no for an answer, even though she'll be sighing the whole time and letting me know what an imposition it all is.

Erin shook her head. Things would have to get a lot worse before she'd consider calling Aunt Noreen.

Lost in thought, Erin jumped when the phone rang. Would it be Annette again? It rang twice more and finally she picked it up. "Hello? Peters residence."

"Hi, honey. It's Dad," her father's voice boomed over the line.

"Oh, Dad, I'm glad to hear your voice."

She listened eagerly as her father told her that Sean couldn't be moved from the hospital in Quebec for a few more days. He sounded preoccupied and Erin could tell he was still worried about her brother, though he reassured her that Sean's leg would eventually heal properly. Taking down the phone numbers of the hospital and the motel where her parents were staying, Erin told him she was doing fine on her own with Abby.

Hanging up, she felt a wave of relief. Her brother was going to be okay. Suddenly she realized that she hadn't called Greg. No time like the present, she told herself—just get it over with.

When Greg's mother answered, Erin said, "Oh, hi, Mrs. Brockton, this is Erin. Can I talk to Greg please?"

She was rehearsing what she wanted to tell him, but Mrs. Brockton said that Greg wasn't home. "In fact, dear, he left yesterday for a few days at the shore with his cousin. I'm so sorry you missed him, but I'll be sure and have him call you when he gets back."

"Oh, don't bother, it wasn't important." Saying good-bye, Erin hung up and stood frowning in concentration. Did this mean that Greg hadn't made those anonymous calls after all? Maybe, but then again, he could have called from another town—there was no way to tell.

Not knowing what to think, Erin locked up the house and set off to pick up Abby.

Standing in the doorway of the classroom, Erin looked at all the children pulling on sweaters and rolling up their paintings to take home. She couldn't see Abby—maybe she had gone to wash her hands or something. Erin edged into the room and as the crowd began to thin out, she approached the teacher who was tying a little boy's shoelace.

"Hi, Mrs. Flynn, where's Abby?"

The woman raised her head and stared at Erin

in surprise. "Oh. I didn't expect to see you," she said, sounding quite puzzled. "Abby's mother already picked her up."

Erin's heart stopped. She couldn't make sense of what the woman was saying. "Her mother?" she managed to say. "What do you mean?"

Mrs. Flynn sent the little boy on his way out the door and stood up. She frowned at Erin in concern. "Why, she came about half an hour ago and said there had been a change in plans. Naturally I assumed you knew about it."

"No, I didn't." Erin's voice sounded strange and faraway in her ears. "Are you sure it was her mother?"

Mrs. Flynn gave her a look of alarm. "Well, I've never met Mrs. Peters before, but that's who she said she was. And Abby seemed to know her."

"Was she tall and thin, with blond hair?" Erin persisted.

"Yes, I thought to myself that Abby looks a lot like her." Mrs. Flynn paused and then added, "Is there something wrong?"

"No," Erin gasped. She felt as if she couldn't breathe. "No, it's just a misunderstanding." She turned and almost ran out the door.

As she stood in the bright spring sunshine, a rush of confused panic swept over her. How could she have let this happen? She had lost the little girl she was supposed to be taking care of. And what should she do to find her?

Go home to the Peters house and call Annette, she decided. Frantic, she began half-walking, half-running along the sidewalk. She had to get back and call as fast as she could.

Her hands didn't seem to work properly as she fumbled with the key, but at last she was inside. In the kitchen she snatched up the phone and then dialed the number she had written on the message for Mr. Peters. How long ago it seemed—had it been only Saturday when Annette had first called?

She heard the ringing begin and for the first time wondered what she was actually going to say to Annette. How can I persuade her to let me come and pick up Abby, wherever she is? But the ringing kept on and on, and finally Erin had to admit that letting it continue wasn't going to accomplish anything.

Hanging up abruptly, she found she couldn't keep still. As she paced back and forth across the kitchen, aimlessly moving various items from the table to the countertop and back again, her thoughts were racing. What else should she do besides trying to phone Annette? Maybe I can find out somehow where she lives and drive over there and talk to her in person, she thought. Erin grasped at this idea, but then she realized that if Annette wasn't answering the phone, she probably wasn't home. What would be the point of driving to an empty house?

"How could I let this happen?" Erin's hands twisted together in anguish as she spoke this thought aloud. And poor little Abby—what must she be thinking? The last thing I said to her was that I'd pick her up after school. The memory brought tears to Erin's eyes.

She dialed Annette's number again and listened as it rang and rang. Hanging up at last, she thought, maybe I should call Mr. Peters and tell him what's happened.

But how could she tell him Abby was gone and she had no idea where the child and her mother were? Maybe they're still on their way to Annette's house. I'll keep calling every ten minutes—she's just got to be there!

But Erin found she couldn't wait for ten minutes between calls, and she kept dialing the number at shorter and shorter intervals. Each time she replaced the receiver, terrible thoughts flashed across her mind. What if Annette had decided to take Abby on the vacation she'd been talking about? They could be on their way to anywhere! She remembered a TV show she'd seen in which a man had kidnapped his child from his ex-wife and the two of them hadn't been found for ten years. Such things did happen.

When half an hour had passed and her calls to Annette were still unanswered, Erin decided she had to let Mr. Peters know. On his desk she found the paper with the string of numbers he'd written down. It felt strange to simply push a few buttons and know that she'd be talking to someone halfway around the globe. But when the hotel operator answered, Erin discovered that Mr. Peters was not in the hotel. Perhaps he was still out in the country looking at building sites—the operator didn't know. Leaving a message that he should call her, Erin hung up.

She had dreaded telling Mr. Peters her story, but being unable to reach him left Erin feeling alone, cut off from the ordinary world. Hopelessly she lifted the receiver to try Annette once more and stood listening to the ringing tone.

Suddenly it was cut off in mid-ring and Erin heard the unmistakable hollow sound of an open line. No one spoke, however, and after a moment Erin said carefully, "Hello? Is that Mrs. Peters?"

She was clutching the phone so hard that her hand ached as she heard a kind of sob. Then Annette said, "You can't take my baby away from me. I won't let you!"

"Mrs. Peters, please, let me talk to Abby." But Erin's desperate plea was met with a decisive click as Annette hung up.

Oh, God, what shall I do? Breathless now but...
Who can I ask for help? There was no one except
calling her aunt and uncle—until could she get
from Queenie? The babe suspected something—
could come downstairs to tell the other servants
had stretched out beside and in their underwear,
when it truly shine and seen up the bedroom.
Could Angela have thought her lunder clothes
Abby call into the night. "Where is Angela now?"

"Is this Abby," an unfamiliar woman's voice
inquired.

"Yes, it is..."

"Are you Abby Peters's babysitter?"

"Yes. Why?" But she cautioned. "What is it?"
she wondered.

"Well, my name is Ruth Dobbs and I was—
Abby here at the moment?"

CHAPTER SEVEN

Oh, God, what shall I do? Erin thought wildly. Who can I ask for help? There was no point in calling her mom and dad—what could they do from Quebec? The only course of action she could come up with was to call the police. She had stretched out her hand to pick up the phone when it rang. Erin snatched up the receiver. Could Annette have changed her mind and let Abby call her?

"Is this Erin?" an unfamiliar woman's voice inquired.

"Yes, it is."

"Are you Abby Peters's baby-sitter?"

"Yes. Why?" Erin was confused. What now? she wondered.

"Well, my name is Ruth Dobbs and I have Abby here with me now."

Before the woman could go on, Erin almost shouted into the phone, "What? Is she okay?"

"Yes, she is," the woman said in a disapproving voice. "I was walking my dog in the woods near our house and I found the child wandering around all by herself. It's lucky she knows her home phone number."

Erin could hardly believe what the woman was saying. "Oh, thank God. I've been so worried—I didn't know what to do. . . ." She realized that in her relief she was babbling and said in a more controlled voice, "Thank you so much for calling. I'll come and pick her up right away. Where are you?"

The woman explained how to get to her house, which was several miles away. Then she said coldly, "I think her parents had better be informed."

"I've already put in a call to her father," Erin assured her. "He's out of the country on business and what happened was that Abby's mother picked her up at nursery school without letting me know. I haven't been able to reach Mrs. Peters and I've been absolutely frantic."

In a much friendlier tone, Mrs. Dobbs said to Erin, "Oh, I see. Well, don't you worry. Abby will be here with me when you get here."

"Thanks so much," Erin said. "But could I

speak to Abby for a minute? I guess I can hardly believe that she's really all right.''

Erin waited breathlessly and soon she heard Abby's small voice at the other end of the line. ''Hi, Erin. I didn't want to stay at my mother's house.''

''That's okay, honey. I'm coming right over to pick you up and bring you home.'' Erin was almost in tears as Abby replied, ''Okay. But come soon, Erin.''

Weak with relief, Erin leaned her forehead against the kitchen wall for a moment. Thank God, she's safe. The thought kept repeating itself in her mind as she grabbed her purse and the keys to Mr. Peters's car.

Abby must have been watching from the front window, because when Erin pulled into Mrs. Dobbs's driveway, the door opened and Abby rushed down the steps.

Erin jumped out of the car and when the little girl raced into her arms, she held the small body fiercely to her. At last Abby wriggled out of her embrace. Erin brushed her sleeve hastily across her eyes as the two of them walked toward the little house.

Mrs. Dobbs was standing at the front door.

''Hello, Erin,'' she said. ''I'm Mrs. Dobbs. Come on inside.''

Erin smiled in reply. She wasn't sure she

could trust herself to speak yet. But Abby seemed perfectly okay. "I had some milk and cookies," she confided. Then she looked at Mrs. Dobbs. "Can I have one more cookie?"

Mrs. Dobbs patted the child's head. "Certainly, honey. You know where the cookie jar is."

As Abby trotted into the kitchen, Erin said, "Mrs. Dobbs, I don't know how to thank you. I couldn't imagine what had happened and I was so terribly worried and upset. I'm just so glad you were there to—" Erin's voice broke.

Mrs. Dobbs patted her arm consolingly. "Well, dear, I'm glad I was there, too. And everything has turned out all right after all. But I was upset myself when I found her. She said she was on her way home. But of course, there she was in the middle of the woods, nowhere near anyplace that could have been her home. So I told her I'd take her to my house and call her mother. I must tell you, I was surprised when she said 'No!' in a kind of scared voice, and then she said she wanted me to call you. Naturally that's what I did, and then when you explained what had happened . . ." Her voice trailed off and she gave Erin an inquiring look.

Ignoring Mrs. Dobbs's obvious wish to know more about Abby's family, Erin said quickly, "I don't really understand how Abby ended up in the woods myself, but thank goodness you came along when you did.'' Then she asked, "Has Abby seemed upset or anything?''

"No, not exactly. But she has been very quiet. Of course I asked her why she was in the woods by herself, but she just said she didn't know and I couldn't get much more than that out of her.''

Abby came into the room and stood next to Erin. Giving the child's hand a reassuring squeeze, Erin said to Mrs. Dobbs, "I think we'd better be going home. I just can't thank you enough for everything you've done.''

"I'm glad I was able to help,'' Mrs. Dobbs told her. "Good-bye, Abby dear.''

" 'Bye,'' the child said shyly.

Abby was silent on the way home and Erin didn't push her to talk. But once they were inside the Peters house, she asked gently, "Abby, can you tell me what happened after your mother picked you up at school?''

"We went to my mommy's house,'' Abby said slowly. "And I had some lunch but I didn't like it. It was tomato soup and she didn't have any crackers or anything.'' Abby paused and didn't seem to know what else to say. Then she looked at Erin. "Can I sit on your lap?''

Without replying, Erin sat on the couch and held out her arms. When Abby had climbed up into her lap, Erin held her close. "What happened after lunch, Abby?'' She felt the stiffness in the child's body and thought, I feel awful, making her tell me all about it. But I have to know, and I have to be able to tell Mr. Peters.

''Mommy kept on talking to me,'' Abby said at last, so softly that Erin could hardly hear her.

''What was she talking about?'' Erin asked quietly.

''Babies, I think. She was talking about her baby, but I don't think she has a baby, does she?'' When Erin shook her head, Abby went on, ''So I didn't know where the baby was. And then once I said I wanted to go home and she said I was home already. But I wasn't.'' Erin's arms tightened around Abby as the little girl said haltingly, ''I don't know what else she was saying. I couldn't get it and Mommy sounded sort of mad.''

Erin held her for a few moments without speaking. Then she said, ''Abby, how did you get into the woods where Mrs. Dobbs found you?''

''I was walking home,'' Abby said, as if it should be obvious. Then she added, ''Mommy went to get me some ice cream, I think. She locked the door and she said I couldn't go home. But I wanted to. So I opened the other door—the glass one in the living room and I started to walk home. I thought I would come to our fence real soon. But I didn't.''

Erin shivered. If Mrs. Dobbs hadn't happened along, Abby might still be wandering alone and terrified in the large undeveloped tract of woodland that stretched for miles on the far side of town. "Oh, Abby," she said.

Abby's lower lip trembled as she stared at Erin. "I didn't want to stay at my mommy's house," she whispered. "She said I had to, but I wanted to go home."

"That's okay, Abby, you're home now."

By dinnertime Erin still felt drained from the emotional upheaval of the day. She couldn't face the idea of cooking a proper meal, but Abby seemed perfectly content with scrambled eggs and toast. Afterward they sat together on the couch in the living room to watch TV. When the show was over, Erin took Abby upstairs and got her settled in bed with her teddy.

She perched on the edge of the child's bed, stroking her hair for several minutes until Abby fell asleep, and on her way downstairs Erin realized that she'd taken every opportunity to touch the little girl ever since she'd picked her up at Mrs. Dobbs's house. I must be afraid she'll disappear again, she thought. Then she told herself firmly, don't be an idiot—nothing else is going to happen. In the living room she flopped wearily on the couch and gazed blankly at the detective show on the screen.

What an incredible day, she thought. She was overwhelmed with relief at having Abby back, but she couldn't stop thinking about what had happened. It was almost impossible to believe that Annette had really kidnapped Abby—Erin couldn't take it in. It had never occurred to her that people she knew could do such terrible things. And Mr. Peters had never explained that he and Annette had problems concerning Abby— Erin had had no warning that the child's mother might be driven to such action.

What was Annette thinking now? She must be frantic, not knowing what had become of Abby after she'd left the child locked in her house. I guess I should try calling Annette again, Erin thought wearily. I'll just rest for a minute first. She'd dialed Annette's number several times during the afternoon, but there had been no answer and Erin didn't know any other way to get hold of her. I'm really not looking forward to talking with her again, Erin admitted to herself, but I can't let her go on wondering whether her child is safe.

It's lucky I didn't reach Mr. Peters when I called earlier, Erin thought. At least when he gets my message and calls back, I won't have to tell him Abby's missing. But, of course, I will have to explain to him what happened. I'm sure he'll be really angry. How could Annette have done such a thing?

The phone rang and as Erin went into the study to answer it, she gathered her thoughts. It was no doubt Mr. Peters returning her call, and she'd have to be as brief and collected as she could. "Hello, Peters residence," she said into the receiver.

But it wasn't Mr. Peters. The voice on the other end was Annette's. "I want my baby back. They've taken my baby again," she said shrilly. "They're always trying to take my baby from me."

Erin firmly interrupted her. "Mrs. Peters, Abby is here now and she's fine. There's no need to get upset—no one took her away." There was no use in going into what had really happened and it wouldn't help to point out that Annette was the one who had taken Abby. The woman was obviously out of control.

"I knew it!" Annette's voice was ragged. "He's taken my baby away. He's always trying to take my baby from me. . . ."

"Mrs. Peters. Did you hear what I said?" Erin demanded sharply. "Abby is here and she's perfectly safe. She's here at home right now."

"You can't do that!" Annette screamed into the phone. "You took her away. You took my baby. And I want her back. Do you hear me? You can't have my baby!'' Erin tried to break in, but the woman's hysterical voice overrode hers as Annette spewed out her accusations in an unending stream. Finally Erin lowered the receiver and broke the connection.

Hugging herself and trembling, Erin moved out of the study. What had happened to Annette? The memory of her ranting voice echoed in Erin's ears.

The television was still on and she stood there, watching the rest of the local news. The announcer was saying, ''And there's still no word on the whereabouts of the two men who escaped yesterday from the state prison. It's believed, however, that they may now be driving a blue Ford van which was stolen at gunpoint in the early hours of this morning in North Rockville. Police have issued a warning to residents nearby that these men are armed and dangerous. However, it is believed that they may be heading west . . .'' Just what I need to hear, Erin said to herself as she switched off the set.

She wandered around the living room unable to decide what she wanted to do—read a book? Leaf through the magazines on the coffee table? Fix herself some warm milk? This is silly, she finally realized. I'm totally exhausted. The best thing I can do is go to bed.

After making sure the front door was locked, she turned off the lights and then went into the kitchen to check the back door. It, too, was securely locked. Turning off the light, Erin glanced through the kitchen window into the back yard. Something was moving! Her heart pounding, she edged closer to the window and peered out into the dim yard. It was Abby's swing, swaying gently to and fro.

Clutching the edge of the window, Erin thought, it must have been the wind. But the trees were still, their leaves barely rustling. Then her eye caught a movement in the bushes near the back fence. Who was out there? Who had brushed against the swing, setting it in motion and betraying his presence?

Finally Erin switched on the outdoor light, but the bushes remained in shadow. The swing was motionless now, and she couldn't see anything at all unusual in the yard. It was someone's dog, or a raccoon or something, bumping into the swing while it chased another animal, she told herself sternly. You're imagining things—just get to bed.

But once in her room with the lights off, Erin lay awake, her eyes wide open. Every time she closed them, she heard strange scary noises—rustling in the bushes, scratching sounds near the house, unexplained creaks and thuds. I know there really is no one skulking around the house, she thought. These noises are just ordinary night sounds—I wouldn't pay any attention to them if I weren't so keyed up already. Just close your eyes and keep them closed. You'll go right to sleep.

But her mind raced on. What if I'm so tired that I don't wake up if anything happens? I'd better sleep by the phone in Mr. Peters's room. And Abby can sleep there with me. With a rush of nervous energy, she went into the little girl's room and gathered her up. Abby opened her eyes and muttered something as Erin carried her to the big bed, but as soon as she was under the covers she turned over and was fast asleep again.

Erin glanced around the room. She couldn't think of anything more she could do to protect herself and Abby, and she found herself wishing that the Jensens' big black dog, Thor, were here in the house to lie across the bedroom doorway. With a sigh she climbed into bed next to the little girl and closed her eyes in exhaustion.

CHAPTER EIGHT

Erin slept fitfully, waking several times during the night. And when morning finally came, she still felt worn out. She opened her eyes to find Abby staring at her with a puzzled expression. "Why are we sleeping in my dad's bed?" she asked.

"Well, I thought your dad might call during the night and I wanted us to be near the phone." It sounded like a feeble excuse, but Abby seemed to accept it.

"Did he call?" she asked innocently, and when Erin said, "No," the little girl stretched and then got up and pattered into the bathroom.

Erin herself felt reluctant to leave the cozy shelter of the big bed. She'd expected her fears of last night to seem foolish in the light of day, but instead she found herself still fighting a vague sense of dread.

When she'd finally made herself get up and dressed, she called to Abby, "I'm going down to start breakfast."

What am I really afraid of? Erin asked herself. The answer was clear—it was Annette. What if she tried to take Abby again? I couldn't stand it, Erin thought. But she knew the possibility was all too real.

I can't let Abby go to nursery school today. There's no way for me to prevent Annette from picking up her own child—I don't have any authority to tell the teacher she's not allowed to do it. I'll just call the school and say Abby's staying home today.

The decision should have been a relief, but Erin felt just as jumpy and unsettled as before. It was silly, she knew, but she just couldn't get rid of the nagging fear that something bad was going to happen in the Peters house. Actually, things were better in a sense. Whoever was making the weird phone calls—whether it was Greg or someone else—seemed to have given up. And though she'd thought someone was lurking in the yard last night, it had obviously been her imagination—no one had tried to break in.

The water in the kettle was boiling and Erin

began pouring it into the coffee filter. So you see, there's nothing to worry about except Annette, and she can't really be planning to break into this house to steal Abby. Unconvinced, the other half of her mind replied stubbornly, someone *did* break in sometime—the person who ripped up the photograph.

Erin froze as the realization flashed across her mind. No one had broken into the house—there was no sign at all of a break-in. That's why I thought for a while it might have been Dan, because he had a key. A shudder ran through her as the logical conclusion presented itself. The person who ripped up the photograph was Annette. Of course. She must still have a key to the house she'd once lived in!

Abby came to sit at the table and Erin somehow got through breakfast on automatic pilot. Her brain was churning, and her conviction grew stronger. They had to get out of that house.

As she cleared the table, Erin said brightly, "Guess what, Abby? I have a great idea. Instead of going to nursery school today, I'm going to take you over to my house. In fact, we'll make it a sleep-over. How does that sound?"

"Goody!" Abby grinned. "I'm going to go up and get my toothbrush and my nightie and my bear."

Anxious to remove both of them from what now seemed an even more perilous situation, Erin went upstairs, too, and threw her things into her bag. Impelled by a sense of urgency, she helped Abby collect a few clothes for the next day. Stopping only to snatch up the paper with Mr. Peters's phone number and the numbers for her parents in Quebec, she hustled the little girl out the door and into the car.

"I thought we were going to walk," Abby said in surprise. "We did last time."

"I know," Erin replied, "but now we have our stuff to carry and it might get too heavy."

But Erin admitted to herself that that wasn't the real reason. Now that she felt certain Annette had let herself into the Peters house on Sunday and had torn up the photo of Abby and her father, Erin thought the woman must be capable of anything. What if she were lurking around the corner at this very moment, ready to drag Abby into her car? It sounded absurd, but Erin knew she wouldn't feel safe until she and Abby were in Erin's own house. Then Annette wouldn't know where to find them.

Her parents had left their car in the airport parking lot, so Erin drove Mr. Peters's car into the garage. As she let herself and Abby into the house, its comforting familiarity surrounded her. Here she felt secure.

Abby had already run upstairs to Erin's room and was looking around at all the things she'd examined when she was there before. Erin followed her and realized that after they'd fooled around with her costume jewelry and looked at the pictures on her bulletin board, she didn't have much else for Abby to play with. Had her mother kept any of her old games or toys?

"Come on, Abby," she said to the child. "We're going to go up to the attic and see if we can find some of my old toys."

Sure enough, they discovered Erin's old Barbie doll and Abby was delighted.

Let's see, Erin thought as they went back downstairs. What are we going to do about meals? She knew there must be something in the house for lunch, and maybe she'd take Abby out for a pizza for dinner. I'll have to get some groceries sometime, she told herself, but that can wait. However, she knew she'd better get hold of her parents and Mr. Peters today. If either of them phoned the Peters house during the daytime and didn't get an answer, that wouldn't present a problem. But if her mom and dad tried to reach her or if Mr. Peters returned her call at night, they'd be worried when no one was home.

Erin would just say that she'd gotten lonely in the big old house and had decided that it would be a treat for Abby to have a sleep-over. That way, her parents wouldn't be alarmed. She realized that she'd have to tell Mr. Peters what had been happening. She couldn't simply pretend to him that she'd moved herself and Abby to her house just for fun. He had a right to know that his daughter was in danger of being kidnapped by his ex-wife. And besides, it would be a relief to share this problem with the only person who could do anything about it.

Feeling organized and efficient, Erin decided to try calling Mr. Peters after lunch, before it got too late. If he still wasn't there, she could leave a message and give him the phone number at her house. Then she would phone her parents this evening. Maybe they would know for sure when they were coming home.

At that moment the phone rang in her parents' bedroom, startling Erin. Then she smiled. All that thinking about phone calls must have made it ring! It was probably some friend of her mother's who didn't know about Sean's accident.

Abby was still engrossed in Barbie's wardrobe as Erin crossed the hall and picked up the phone. "Hello?"

Her heart sank as she recognized Annette's voice. "You have to give me my baby. I'm going to come and get her and bring her back to my house, and then we'll be good and we'll be happy.''

Erin was dumbfounded. How had Annette found her? And what could she say to head Annette off? Speaking quietly so Abby wouldn't hear her, she said, "Oh, you can't, Mrs. Peters, Abby's at nursery school right now. But I'll tell you what. I'll bring her to your house when school is over, okay?''

"Yes, Erin, you do that. I'll be waiting." Erin heard the click as Annette hung up.

A chill ran down Erin's spine. Annette had sounded coldly determined, and completely in control this time. But the way she never said Abby's name but always just called her "my baby" gave Erin the creeps—it was almost as if the little girl was only a doll, not a real person.

One thing was certain: Erin had no intention of taking Abby to Annette's house, but they couldn't stay here either. They'd have to find another, safer place to go, where Annette would never find them. And they'd have to leave right away.

Where could they go? Erin wished desperately that her parents were home. She'd never felt so alone in her life. Then her dad's words echoed in her head—"If you have any problems, you can always call your Aunt Noreen." And as awful as Aunt Noreen was, Erin felt she'd give a lot right now to see her disapproving face.

Erin tiptoed across the hall and peeked in the doorway of her room. Abby was still on the floor playing with the doll. Satisfied that the little girl was content for the moment, Erin crept back to her parents' room and with shaking hands fumbled through the pages of her mother's address book. She dialed the number and thought about what she was going to say.

But the phone shrilled on and on without an answer. Grasping at straws, Erin thought, maybe I dialed wrong. She tried again and this time she had to admit that Aunt Noreen wasn't home.

Erin sank down on her parents' bed, twisting her hands in her lap. What was she going to do now? She guessed she could call one of her parents' many friends in the neighborhood, but it would be hard to explain everything that had happened. And besides, Erin felt she had to take Abby farther away. Annette had tracked them to Erin's house, and if she was that determined, she'd be able to find Abby anywhere in her own old neighborhood. After all, the child couldn't be kept locked in a house forever. Aunt Noreen would have been perfect—she lived in Broomfield, about an hour away.

Think, Erin, she told herself. There must be someplace you can go. Then it came to her. She could take Abby to Mr. Peters's cabin in the Berkshires. It would certainly be far enough away. And Dan was staying there. He'd be an ally, and the best one she could have, since he was part of Abby's family.

Now she just had to get herself and Abby there before Annette discovered that the child wasn't at school. Erin had seen an envelope with the key to the cabin and a hand-drawn map of how to get there in Mr. Peters's desk. Though she hated the idea of returning to that house, she'd have to go and get it, and she'd also need the cash Mr. Peters had left for her.

Taking a deep breath, Erin thought, okay, let's get moving. There was no time to explain things to Abby—she'd worry about that later. Walking into her own room, she said, "Abby, we're going to go for a long ride in the car. You can take Barbie with you if you want. Pack up all her things—we have to go right away."

Erin picked up her own bag that she'd brought back from the Peters house, as well as the one she'd packed for Abby, and they went downstairs and out to the car.

The little girl seemed to realize that now was not the time for questions. When they pulled up in front of Abby's house, she merely nodded after Erin told her, "I'm just going in for a minute and I'll be right back. I'm locking the car doors—don't open them for anybody.''

Hurrying into the house, Erin grabbed the money from the desk drawer and made sure the map and key were both in the envelope. She shoved them into her purse and then ran up the stairs, taking them two at a time. Abby might need a jacket in the mountains. She snatched the first warm garment she found and raced back down to the first floor. She was out of breath when she reached the car.

Glancing around to make sure Annette wasn't lying in wait, Erin unlocked the car door and got in behind the wheel. Make sure you relock all the doors, she instructed herself—it was hard to keep calm and to think like a fugitive. She put the car in gear and then made herself take time to give Abby a reassuring smile. "Okay, honey, we're off."

CHAPTER NINE

The first part of the directions to the Peters cabin sounded perfectly simple—all Erin had to do was get on the Mass. Pike heading west. But even though Erin had lived in the greater Boston area all her life and had been on the turnpike often with her parents, finding the entrance to it wasn't so easy. She ended up on Route 128 going the wrong way and had to get off and ask for directions at a gas station.

By the time she'd finally reached the entrance and had gotten her toll ticket from the machine, Erin was beginning to wonder if she'd made the right decision after all. Maybe I should have gone to a motel somewhere and waited for Mr. Peters to get home, she thought. But how could I have explained that to Abby? The little girl had been shuttled around so much already, and at least Erin could make an adventure out of "going to visit Dan at the cabin."

After half an hour or so, Abby asked, "When are we going to have lunch, Erin? I'm hungry."

With a shock of surprise Erin realized that she'd been so intent on getting out of Annette's reach that she hadn't even thought about food. "Of course you are, honey," she said. "We'll stop at the next restaurant I see."

In another ten minutes she had pulled off the turnpike and was carefully parking the big Lincoln in a space with no other cars next to it. Erin wasn't used to driving such a massive vehicle—it was a lot different from her parents' small Ford.

The turnpike food-and-fuel stop was identical to every other one in the state, but Abby thought it was great. She carefully opened her miniature milk carton while Erin sipped the almost tasteless coffee. After they'd eaten, Abby wanted to look in the gift shop, but Erin was anxious to get back on the road. "We'll pick out a postcard for your dad, but then we have to get going," she told the child. To herself she added, I want to make sure I find the cabin before it gets dark.

In the car she helped Abby buckle herself and her teddy into the seat belt. Then she made sure the directions were in easy reach, and they set off west toward Springfield. Abby was amazed when Erin informed her that she could ask the truckers to toot their horns by making a pulling-down gesture with her hand. As they passed a big semi, Abby tried it out and was thrilled when the driver grinned and obligingly hooted for her.

An hour later, Erin had managed to get through Springfield and onto the four-lane highway that would take them into the Berkshires. She was feeling pretty pleased with herself. After all, she'd never driven this far alone before. But from this point on, the directions said things like "Bear right at Cassidy's dairy farm" and "After sign for reservoir, take second left." The narrow road wound up through the foothills and the "second left" she took turned out to be someone's driveway.

Suddenly noticing that the gas gauge needle showed only a quarter full, Erin pulled into a combination gas station and convenience store. When a girl about her own age came out to fill the tank, Erin asked, "Am I going the right way to Old Hill Road?"

"Old Hill Road?" The girl looked totally blank. "I never heard of it. Let me ask my dad."

Her father, wiping his greasy hands on a rag, did his best to help, but it was clear that he hadn't the faintest idea where the turnoff for the Peters cabin was, and Erin didn't have enough information to give him any hints. At last she thanked them and kept going the same direction she'd been traveling. I've got to come to it sometime, she thought.

"Are we lost?" Abby asked her cautiously as Erin pulled off the road and read over the list of directions once more.

"I guess so." Erin forced a smile. "But we'll find it, don't worry."

"We didn't pass the covered bridge and the duck pond yet," Abby told her. "That's when we're almost there."

Covered bridge? Erin had seen one of those historic marker signs for a covered bridge a couple of miles back. Making a careful U-turn, she drove back the way they'd come and then turned to follow the arrow.

When they found the covered bridge, she said to Abby, "Is this the one you saw before, honey?" And when Abby nodded, Erin went on, "Is it on the same side of the road?"

The little girl looked puzzled and Erin explained, "Which window do you look out of to see it when you come here with your dad?"

The child's face cleared. "Oh, it's always on my side," she said. "I'm the one that watches for it."

Erin smiled at her. "You're a great path-finder, Abby. I'm glad you remembered about the bridge."

After that it took only another ten minutes to find the dirt road to the cabin. Abby was bouncing in her seat as Erin turned off by the mailbox marked Peters and finally pulled into the turn-around behind an old black Porsche.

Abby began to unbuckle her seat belt as Erin leaned back exhausted in her seat. Thank heaven we're here, she thought tiredly. Then she saw the door of the little white house open and Dan step out onto the stoop. He looked puzzled, and when he recognized his father's car, she saw a shadow cross his face.

Pulling herself together, Erin got out of the car and went around to help Abby open the heavy passenger door. Scrambling out, Abby yelled, "Hi, Dan!" and then raced inside the little house.

"What are you doing here?" Dan's question sounded curt and unfriendly, and Erin thought, he doesn't want us to be here. What will we do now?

Aloud she said, "Hi, Dan. I'm sorry to intrude on you, but I didn't know what else to do."

Dan didn't smile as he said, "I guess I don't know what you mean."

Erin glanced through the door of the house and saw that Abby was busy pulling toys out of a cupboard. Since the child was out of earshot, Erin plunged into her explanation. "Annette kidnapped Abby yesterday." Before Dan had a chance to respond, Erin went on, "I won't even go into how I got her back, but I was terrified, and more important, Abby was, too. She doesn't want to be with her mom—she seems almost afraid of her. So I took Abby to my house, but Annette called me there and said she'd take Abby again. I didn't know where to go or what to do, and the only thing I could think of was getting out of there. My parents aren't even home—they're in Quebec with my brother in the hospital, and I had to find somewhere safe for Abby until her dad, I mean your dad, gets home." Erin paused for breath and then added, "I hope you don't mind too much."

Dan looked at her for a moment. "Kidnapped?" It was obvious he didn't believe her. "You must be kidding."

"No, I'm not." Aware that her explanation must have seemed totally disjointed, she tried again. This time, when she got to the part about Abby being found wandering in the woods, Dan said, "Good lord! What a mess." Then he added, "Does anyone know you're here?"

"No," Erin said, "I thought I'd call your

dad when I got here and let him know what's going on.''

"Well, not from right here," Dan replied with a crooked smile. "There's no phone. You'll have to go into town to make a call."

"Oh." Maybe I made a mistake in rushing up here, Erin thought. He sure doesn't look very pleased to see us. His tall body seemed to bar the path to the house, and for a moment she wondered if he would tell her to get back in the car and go away. Then with a flash of annoyance she thought, but it's his family and his stepmother I'm talking about. He should be as concerned as I am—maybe more.

As if he could read her thoughts, Dan gestured toward the house. "Well, as long as you're here, come on in. We'll work something out."

The house was as small as it had looked from outside. Abby had climbed up on the bed in the only bedroom and was introducing her teddy bear to a collection of pinecones and rocks. She obviously felt at home, and she explained to Erin that she'd collected these things with her dad the last time they were there. But the child's eyes were drooping, and she made no protest when Erin tucked her into the double bed with her teddy bear for a nap.

Closing the bedroom door gently, Erin walked into the cabin's main room and sank into an overstuffed armchair in front of the fireplace. She looked up at Dan and said, "I'm really sorry to interfere with your vacation. Believe me, I wouldn't have driven all this way if I'd had any other options."

His expression softened as he gazed down at her. "Hey, it's all right," he said quietly. "But you look wiped out. Why don't you just take it easy for a while? I was about to go out to collect some kindling for the fireplace when you showed up." He moved toward the door. "We'll work things out when I get back, okay?"

Erin managed a weak smile. "Okay." As he walked out the door, she leaned back in the chair and closed her eyes. At last Abby was safe and she could relax—it seemed like ages since she'd been able to feel that. Now all she had to do was call Mr. Peters . . . Before she could finish the thought, she was asleep.

A dark-green Volvo coasted silently along the driveway and came to a stop next to the Lincoln. The tall blond woman slid out from behind the wheel and closed the driver's door cautiously behind her. She cast a quick look around and then walked to the edge of the clearing. Dan's wood-gathering efforts were easy to hear and the woman smiled—he was hard at work and out of sight.

She pushed open the door of the little house.

Erin was fast asleep in the big armchair and the woman crept in quietly, careful not to disturb her. She seemed to know exactly where she was going as she tiptoed across the living area to the bedroom beyond.

In a moment she emerged again, carrying the small form of her sleeping child in her arms. "Shh, baby, don't cry, Mommy's taking you home," she whispered as she slipped outside and laid Abby carefully on the back seat of the Volvo. Covering her with a blanket, she closed the car door and hovered for a moment to be sure the little girl didn't awaken.

Annette stood looking around the clearing. Then, moving quickly, she grabbed a pair of wire clippers from the Volvo's front seat and raised the hood of the big Lincoln. Peering at the massive engine, she snipped through every wire she could see. The Porsche's hood gave her a little trouble, but at last she got it open and again cut through whatever wires and hoses she could reach.

Satisfied, she walked rapidly back to the Volvo. In a moment she had disappeared down the driveway as quietly as she had come.

CHAPTER TEN

Someone was shaking Erin's shoulder, calling her name over and over again. Opening her eyes, she stared into Dan's face. "Wow, I must have been really tired," she said. "I didn't even hear you come back." She stretched and then registered his look of concern. "Is something wrong?"

"Abby's not in the bedroom," he told her. "Do you know where she went?"

"What?" Erin sat bolt upright. Her fears for Abby's safety—the fears she'd thought were banished for good when they'd arrived here—returned full force and for a moment she could hardly think. Then, pushing away her anxiety, she said, "She must have gone outside to play."

"I didn't see her out there as I came in," Dan said dubiously.

Erin scrambled out of the deep chair. "She's got to be around somewhere. I'm going to look."

Outside, the two of them stood looking around the clearing. "Abby!" Erin called. "Where are you?"

Calling the child's name again, Erin walked around the small house. It was obvious that Abby was nowhere nearby, and Erin looked helplessly at the surrounding woods. She turned to Dan. "Where would she go to play?"

"Gosh, I'm not sure. Maybe along the driveway—she knows that's where the blackberry bushes are. Or I guess she could have taken the path down to the creek."

The driveway was the closest place to look. As Erin crossed the turnaround, she caught a glimpse of something on the muddy ground next to the Lincoln. It was Abby's teddy bear! Frowning, she bent to pick him up. What was he doing out here? It wasn't like Abby to take him outside. Brushing him off and propping him on the hood of the car, she thought, maybe she left him here on her way to the blackberries.

By the time they had walked the whole length of the driveway calling Abby's name, Erin had to admit the child wasn't anywhere in hearing distance. A vision of that small figure in the middle of the twisting road, nearly invisible to oncoming drivers, made her catch her breath.

"Do you think she could have gone out into the road?" she asked Dan with worry in her voice.

But he shook his head. "I doubt it—Dad's pretty strict about that. And besides, there's nothing much to see along this road. I think she's probably gone down to the creek."

They retraced their steps and Erin went to the door of the house. She didn't really think the child would be there, but it was just possible that Abby had gone inside and hadn't heard them calling her. It took only a moment to make certain that the house was still empty. Erin turned away, her shoulders slumping in disappointment, and followed Dan down the path that led to the creek.

The ground sloped sharply and Erin was grateful for the roots under the dirt that gave her a foothold here and there. Scrambling and slipping down the hill, they finally reached the wide shallow stream that wound between boulders and tall trees. There was no sign of Abby and no answer to their shouts. Dan climbed out onto the flat rocks that lay in the middle of the flowing water. "Abby! Abby, can you hear me?"

His voice died away and there was no answer. After another look along the creek, he returned to where Erin stood. With a puzzled shrug, he said, "I don't know what to think.

But she's not here. There's no way to walk along these steep banks in either direction, and she wouldn't go into the water—it's still ice cold this early in the year.''

Erin's glance followed his. The late afternoon sun sent only a faint light through the dense woods, but in the fading glow she could see that what Dan said was true. The creek's banks fell off sharply beneath a tangle of roots and saplings, and there was no foothold for a small child's explorations.

Panic threatened to engulf her. Where could Abby have gone? Keeping her voice steady with an effort, she said, ''I guess we'd better go back up the path. Aren't there any other places where she likes to play?''

''I don't know,'' he replied helplessly. ''I've only been up here with her a couple of times.'' After a moment's thought, he went on, ''She must have collected those pinecones somewhere around here, and I know there's a pretty good-sized stand of pines off this path. The thing is, though, it's quite a hike and I'm not sure she could find it on her own. There's no real path to it—you have to know where you're going.''

Instantly in her mind's eye, Erin saw the little girl making her way deeper into the woods, scared and completely lost. ''My God, the poor kid! We've got to look for this pine grove before it gets any later. She must be terrified!''

Dan nodded and set off up the rough hillside. By now he had caught Erin's sense of urgency, and when she slipped at a steep curve in the trail, he reached back for her hand to steady her. As they hurried along, Erin saw that there were lots of inviting openings between the trees. These side trails might eventually peter out, but any one of them could tempt a curious child. We'll never be able to search even this part of the woods, Erin thought in despair.

Every dozen yards or so Erin called Abby's name, her voice growing more and more hoarse. Dan, too, was shouting for the little girl, but when they waited to hear an answer, there was none.

At last Dan stopped where another track branched off from the main path. It was overgrown with young trees and brambly bushes, and he frowned in concentration. ''I think this is the way to the stand of pines,'' he said finally. ''Let's try it, anyway—I'll know pretty soon if it's the wrong path.''

They made their way along the almost invisible trail, pushing aside the branches at eye level and avoiding the worst of the wild raspberry canes that caught at their clothing. Erin was grateful that she'd put on Levi's this morning.

But as she tore her flannel shirt away from the prickly grasping vines, she realized that if Abby had come this way, her little face would be a mass of scratches. Then she thought, if that's the only problem I have to deal with, I'll be so thankful!

Emerging from the underbrush, Erin and Dan stood beneath the towering evergreens that formed the pine grove Dan had described. There were hundreds of fallen cones scattered on the ground— this was certainly where Abby had gathered her collection. But she wasn't here now. Taking a deep breath, Erin shouted again. "Abby! Abby! Tell us where you are!" Her voice cracked as tears came to her eyes.

Brushing her sleeve across her face, she turned away. Suddenly she caught a glimpse of red deeper among the trees and strained her eyes to see what it was. Abby had been wearing a red T-shirt!

Erin shouted, "There she is!" Plunging into the woods, she rushed over the leaf-covered forest floor. There was little undergrowth here to bar her way and she raced pell-mell, keeping her eyes locked on the splash of red color in the distance. Then in the fading light her foot came down hard on a fallen log half hidden under the leaves. She slipped and crashed to the ground, her ankle twisting painfully beneath her.

Hearing her cry out as she fell, Dan hurried toward Erin. But as he bent to help her, she gasped, "Get Abby!" He looked at her for a moment and then turned to follow her frantic gesture.

Erin watched him move rapidly through the trees until he reached the place she'd been heading for. She held her breath in anticipation. But when he turned toward her, shaking his head, and started back alone, her stomach turned over in sickening despair.

"It wasn't her?" Erin whispered as he approached. Her tears spilled over when he shook his head again.

"It was one of those pieces of red cloth they use to mark dead trees that should be cut down," he told her gently. Looking down at her, he added, "Erin, we've got to get help."

She nodded dumbly and then pushed herself up from the ground. Taking a step, she winced as pain shot through her ankle. Dan held her arm while she regained her balance. "You really racked yourself up, didn't you?" he said in concern.

"It's just my ankle," she told him. "I think I can walk on it okay." She took a few more steps, trying to ignore the pain. But even with Dan's arm to lean on, it was hard to go very

fast. And every minute that passed was post-
poning the search for Abby.

Finally Dan stopped and said, "This won't
work. We've got to get some help out here
before it's too dark. I'm going to carry you."

Erin began to protest, but he said simply, "I
can't leave you down here alone. This is the
way it's got to be." His attempt at a smile was
grim. "I know it's not very dignified, but it
works." He swung her up over his shoulder in a
fireman's carry and set off toward the house.

Stopping now and then to shout once more
for Abby, he made his way up the steep path.
Erin's thoughts were a jumble of terrified con-
jecture as she bounced along. What if Abby
fell just like I did? She could be lying uncon-
scious somewhere, unable to answer us. How
can anyone search after it gets dark? How are
we going to find her?

At last they reached the house and Dan set
her down carefully on the front stoop. Erin
smiled at him tremulously. "Thanks—I don't
think I'd have made it on my own. But, Dan,
what are we going to do now?"

"You're going to stay here," he replied deci-
sively, "just in case Abby turns up. Someone
has to be here. I'll drive into town and get a
search party organized. I guess I'll go to the
police—they'll know how to do it."

Erin nodded. ''All right. But hurry! I can't bear to think of her out there.''

''I know.'' Dan touched her cheek. ''I'll be as quick as I can.''

Digging into his pocket for his keys, he ran to his car and slid in behind the wheel. Erin waited for the Porsche's engine to come to life. But nothing happened, and after a moment Dan got out, slamming the car door behind him.

''Damn! I don't know what's wrong with it—it was running great this morning.'' He walked toward her. ''Where are the keys to Dad's car?''

''In my purse.'' She stood up but he had already brushed past her into the house. Returning with her canvas shoulder bag, he thrust it at her. When she found the keys, he took them out of her hand.

''Try not to worry,'' he told her. ''I'll be back as soon as I can.''

He got into the Lincoln and turned the ignition key. Once again, nothing happened. Instead of the expected roar of the big engine, there was only silence.

Bewildered, Erin hobbled toward the car. What could be wrong? Dan got out, his face clouded with anger. Before she could speak, he said, ''This isn't possible.'' The two of them moved around to the front of the car and Dan raised the hood.

It was easy to see what the problem was. She watched in silence as Dan opened the hood of the Porsche and then slammed it shut again.

"What the hell's going on here?" He stared at Erin. "Somebody has messed around with both of these cars."

"But why?" Erin stared back at him. "Who could have done it?"

"I don't know," he said slowly, "but whoever it was didn't want us to be able to leave the house."

"It was Annette." The words were out before Erin could think. "She took Abby!"

Dan began, "That's crazy . . ." but the words died on his lips. "I bet you're right."

He walked over to where she was standing next to the big car. Peering down at the ground, he said, "Look. Another car has been here—you can see the tire tracks in the mud." Looking at Erin, he went on, "She must have come while I was out getting the firewood. You were asleep. She just snuck in and took Abby away."

Erin's heart seemed to stop beating. Of course, that must be what had happened. And while they were searching, Annette had put more and more miles between them and Abby. "Oh, God! And it's all my fault. If I hadn't been so sound asleep, she wouldn't . . ." Don't cry, Erin, she told herself fiercely as the tears welled up in her eyes. There's no time for that.

Dan's strong arm came around her shoulders. "Don't blame yourself, Erin. Annette must be crazy. How could you know she'd follow you up here?" He held her tight against him. "But we have to think what to do now."

"We have to go to the police." Erin pulled away and looked into his dark eyes. "Is that okay with you?" After all, she thought, it's his stepmother we're talking about. How does he feel about this?

But he drew her into his arms. His voice was muffled against her hair. "Of course, what do you think? We've got to find Abby."

CHAPTER ELEVEN

"It's a long walk into town," Dan said. "Maybe it would be better if you—"

"No!" Erin wasn't going to be left behind at the cabin, wondering what was going on. "I can walk," she told him. "I'll be fine."

"Okay," he said. "But wait a minute—I think there are some bandages in the house." He disappeared inside and emerged again with a roll of Ace bandage. "Sit down, I'll try to remember how to do this."

Erin slipped off her sneaker and her sock and obediently extended her foot toward him. His warm hands began to wrap the bandage around her ankle, and she found herself thinking, if this were a different situation, I'd really be enjoying it. But she couldn't dispel the picture of Abby's terror when the child realized she'd been snatched away again by her mother.

At last Dan was satisfied with his emergency first aid, and they started down the driveway toward the road. As they walked along in the direction of town, Dan held out his thumb whenever a car went by. Before long a rattletrap pickup slowed and then stopped ahead of them. Dan ran around to the driver's side.

"Can you give us a lift into town?"

"Sure, son." The gray-haired man and his wife peered curiously at Dan. "Car break down?"

"Um, yeah, and we have to get to the police station as soon as we can." Dan looked at their doubtful faces and added, "There's a little girl who's lost and—"

"Say no more, sonny. Hop in the back and we'll have you there in no time."

Dan helped Erin climb into the back of the truck and soon they were on the main street of the small village. When the pickup stopped in front of the combination village hall and police station, the two of them got out. The driver rolled down his window. "If Sheriff Danvers thinks he needs help, tell him Joe Farmer brought you here. I'll stop on my way back home."

"Thanks a lot." Dan waved and then went inside with Erin. Sheriff Danvers was still in his office and he listened to what they had to say without interrupting.

When they had finished, he leaned forward on his desk and said earnestly, "Look, I know you're upset. Let's just take this one step at a time, okay? You think the little girl is with her mother now, is that right?"

"Yes," Erin told him, "but she doesn't want to be with her. I mean, Mrs. Peters kidnapped Abby—that's why we're so upset."

"Yeah, well, I know that's what you believe. But we don't really know that for sure. I think the first thing to do is make sure she's not out in the woods somewhere." Without waiting for an answer, he picked up his phone. "Nola, get me Charlie Ratchett." In another minute he said into the phone, "Hi, Charlie, it's Ray Danvers. I need you to look for a kid who may have wandered off in the woods up by Old Mill Road. Can you come on over here with the dogs?" He waited and then said, "Good enough."

Hanging up, he told Dan and Erin, "Now that we've got that started, let's look at what else we can do. Do you know where we can reach Mrs. Peters?"

Dan shook his head, but Erin said, "Wait—I think I still have her phone number written down somewhere." She pulled out the paper with Annette's number from her shoulder bag and handed it to the sheriff.

After he'd let it ring for quite a while, it was clear that it wasn't going to be answered. He hung up and asked Dan, "Where'd you say your dad is? Have you tried to get hold of him?"

"No," Dan told him, "we don't have a phone at the cabin. You've got the hotel number, don't you, Erin?"

"Yes, it's right here." Erin fished it out of her bag, glad to be contributing something. She knew they were doing everything that could be done, but she could hardly sit still. Her thoughts kept returning to that frightened little girl, wherever she was by now. Abby was still her responsibility.

After a lot of delay, Sheriff Danvers succeeded in reaching Mr. Peters's hotel. The switchboard operator told him that Mr. Peters had checked out earlier in the day, and she had no idea where he had gone.

Hanging up once more, the sheriff said, "Well, kids, let me explain the problem as I see it. If this little girl has been taken away by her mother, there's just not a whole lot I can do. I'm not saying it's right, and of course you're real worried and upset, but the fact is, the woman is her mother. Even if I found her, I couldn't take the child back."

Erin burst out, "But Abby doesn't want to be with her! There's got to be some way to—"

Dan put his hand on her arm. "Hold on, Erin." To Sheriff Danvers he said, "But can you at least find out if Abby is with her mother? Then we'll know she's not out in the woods somewhere."

The sheriff nodded. "I know how you feel, and I'll do as much as I can. I can call the Wentworth police and ask them to go to Mrs. Peters's house—if she's there, they can establish whether the child is with her and let me know. And I'll alert the state police. I don't suppose you know what kind of car she drives?" When Dan and Erin shook their heads, he went on, "Well, they can find that out and put out an APB for her. Of course, you understand that the most they can do is ascertain whether she's got the little girl with her—they can't detain her for driving somewhere with her own kid."

As Erin was still trying to accept this unwelcome reality, the outer door of the police station opened. "Ray?" a gravelly voice called. "I'm here."

"Yo, Charlie, come on in," the sheriff called.

The man who entered seemed to fill the small office. Tall and broad-shouldered, with a mass of iron-gray hair, he exuded strength and confidence. He shook Dan's hand when the sheriff introduced them, and nodded politely to Erin. After Sheriff Danvers had explained the situation, he said to them, "Don't you worry. If the little girl is out in the woods somewhere, Belle and MaryAnn will find her."

Belle and MaryAnn? Who were they? Erin stood up, anxious to get going. But Dan said, "Sheriff, I've got another problem. Both of our cars have been vandalized, we think by Abby's mother. And we can't be stuck at the cabin with no phone and no way to get into town. Is there somewhere I could rent a car—"

Charlie Ratchett broke in. Staring shrewdly at Dan, he said, "I know who you are now. You're John Peters's son." When Dan nodded, Charlie went on, "He's a fine man. I got a car I can loan you until yours gets fixed. Come on, we'll pick it up on the way to your place."

Dan smiled his thanks as they headed for the door. Sheriff Danvers said, "I'll get on with these calls, and I'll send someone out to let you know as soon as we hear anything. Or I'll drive out myself." He looked at Erin's strained expression. "Keep your chin up, honey; I'm sure it'll all work out okay."

Outside, Charlie gestured them to his pickup truck. In the back, two enormous slobbering dogs wriggled an enthusiastic welcome. Erin had never seen real bloodhounds before, and she wasn't sure if she was supposed to pat them or say hello when Charlie said, "This one's Belle and the other one's MaryAnn—the two best trackers I've ever owned." As he swung up into the truck's cab, he told the dogs, "Take it easy, girls, we're not there yet."

They bumped along the road and pulled into a wide driveway. In front of a big open garage, Charlie stopped. "See that Ford station wagon over there? You can use that one—the key's in the visor. Jump in and I'll follow you to your cabin."

Getting down from the truck's cab, Dan helped Erin out and she limped after him to the car. As they drove toward the Peters cabin, she looked out at the gathering dusk. "I wish I could believe Abby did get lost in the woods," she told Dan quietly. "Then the dogs would find her and everything would be all right."

The big man and his massive animals had given her the feeling that they could work miracles. If only Abby had simply wandered away from the cabin! But the destruction to the cars' engines and the extra set of tire tracks in front of the house couldn't be explained away. Erin knew in her bones that Annette had stolen the child, and she had slept and let it happen.

Staring out at the darkness, Erin felt tears sliding down her cheeks. "Wherever she is, she's feeling lost and scared," she murmured. "If only she's where the dogs can find her—" She tried to swallow the lump in her throat. "Oh, Dan, if she's not, how can we save her?"

He reached over and squeezed her hand. "We'll find her, Erin. One way or the other we'll find her."

When they got to the cabin, Charlie said to Erin, "I need something that belongs to the child—a piece of her clothing that she's worn recently."

Erin replied uncertainly, "She's wearing the clothes she put on this morning—her other things are all clean." She paused and then remembered the teddy bear she'd found abandoned in the mud. It still sat on the hood of the Lincoln where she'd put it.

Wordlessly she pointed to it. Charlie said, "That'll do fine." He scooped up the toy and held it down for the dogs to sniff. "Find, Belle! Find, MaryAnn!"

The two huge creatures circled the cars for a few moments and then ran, noses down, toward the house. Dan opened the door and they charged inside, stopping at the bed where Abby had napped that afternoon. Wheeling around, they both trotted purposefully back to the Lincoln and sat, panting and looking expectantly at Charlie.

Letting his dogs sniff the teddy bear again, the tall man walked toward the edge of the clearing where the path went down to the creek. When he called Belle and MaryAnn, they went to him, but as soon as he told them to find Abby, they returned to the car. Once again they followed the trail only they could discern, into the house and back out to the car.

"Well, that's it," Charlie said to Dan and Erin. "The little girl didn't go anywhere except between the house and the car. You can be sure she wasn't out there at all." He waved a big hand toward the surrounding woods.

"She walked into the house when we got here," Erin told him.

"And then maybe she walked back out to that car and maybe she didn't—someone might have carried her out. Didn't you say there was another car? But anyway, one thing's for certain. She didn't set foot anywhere else, or my girls would have told me." He handed the teddy bear to Erin. "I'm sorry we couldn't find her for you," he said quietly. "I hope you'll have news of her soon. On my way home I'll stop and tell Ray Danvers we had no luck."

Waving away their thanks, he motioned the bloodhounds into the truck and soon they had disappeared down the driveway. As the truck's taillights vanished, Erin thought feverishly, there must be something else we can do! I'll go crazy if we have to just sit and wait.

Inside the little house, Dan turned on the lights. "Come and sit down, Erin," he urged. "You're not doing any good pacing around and making your ankle worse."

Still clutching Abby's bear, Erin sank down on the couch but she couldn't relax. Her mind was racing, searching for any possible action they could take. "Do you believe that Annette has Abby?" she asked at last.

Dan nodded. "It's the only thing that makes sense," he replied unhappily.

Burying her face in her hands, Erin saw again Abby's pitiful look when she'd asked Erin if she had to go back to her mother's house. She heard again the child's whimpers during the night. Raising her head, she stared at Dan with a haunted expression. "I'm afraid," she whispered. A violent shudder ran through her body.

In a moment he was sitting beside her, his strong arm around her shoulders. "I know," he said soothingly. "We'll think of something." He turned her face toward him and gently smoothed away the tears from her cheeks. "Come on, Erin, you can't break down now. This won't do Abby any good." Pulling her closer, his hand covered hers and one by one he teased open her clenched fingers. "We're both strung out and exhausted—I think we need some food before we collapse. There's nothing more we can do right now. I'm going to take you to the diner up the road, and after we eat we'll figure out what to do next."

Erin gave him a look of panic. "But what if—"

"Shh, don't worry, I'll leave a note so Sheriff Danvers can find us if he needs to."

Numb and sick at heart, Erin let him lead her out to the car. She still held Abby's teddy bear and as they drove, she peered out into the darkness as if she might catch a glimpse of a little girl with blond hair. Almost in a trance, she walked with Dan into the brightly lit restaurant and sat passively as he ordered for both of them.

When their food arrived, Erin discovered that she was hungrier than she'd thought. They ate in silence for a few minutes. Then Erin said, "I don't think the police will find Annette at her house. Abby ran away from there once. I can't imagine that Annette would try to take her back to the same place again. She'll find somewhere else this time. But where?"

"There are a million places she could go." Dan sounded impatient. "She could hole up in a motel someplace, or she could go to Boston and hide out there—who can guess what she'd do? For all I know, she could go to her family's old home and barricade the doors!''

Erin stared at him. ''What family home?''

A look of surprise crossed his face. ''I just this minute remembered it. It can't be too far from here—we all drove up from the cabin to see it one day.''

''Where is it?'' Erin's voice was insistent.

But Dan shook his head. ''Forget it. It's just a big old mansion that's falling apart, and the grounds are all overgrown. Nobody's lived there for years—it's a wreck.''

''But Annette grew up there?'' When Dan nodded, Erin went on with certainty, ''Then that's it! That's where she'd go to hide—she feels safe there. Oh, Dan, where is it?'' His blank look filled her with despair. ''Think, Dan! What town is it in? You've got to remember!''

He rubbed his hand over his eyes. ''It's just across the New York state line,'' he said slowly. ''And it has a name—it's called Stoner House. She told us the reason for that. Her mother's family was named Stoner and there's a reservoir named after them too. Stoner Reservoir.''

''That's good enough, we can find it!'' Erin couldn't wait to leave. ''Don't you see, that's where she is—that's where Abby is!''

CHAPTER TWELVE

As he got into the borrowed Ford, Dan looked at Erin. "This is crazy," he told her. "I don't even know which road to get on. All I know is it's west of here. We'll end up driving around in circles all night."

Erin had been rummaging through the glove compartment and now she held up a map. It was tattered and worn through at the folds, but her expression was triumphant. "We just have to find the reservoir and we'll know which way to go!" Opening it to the portion that showed the western edge of Massachusetts, she peered at the spiderweb of lines, looking for the little blue oval of a reservoir.

Dan watched her for a moment in silence. Then, still without a word, he got out of the car and went around to the back. Lifting the tailgate, he reached in and returned to the front seat with a square lantern-style flashlight. "I thought I'd noticed this in that box of stuff in the back," he said. "Now if the batteries work—"

He flicked the switch and a bright beam shone on the map. His head close to Erin's, his eyes followed where her finger pointed. "Here's where we are now," she told him.

Dan bent even closer to the map. "I'm trying to remember where we crossed the state line," he said. "I think it must have been right here, near High River. Let's see, if we follow the road from High River into New York, what do we come to? Look, this must be it—does that say Stoner Reservoir?"

Squinting at the tiny blue letters, Erin said finally, "Yes, it does! Oh, Dan, I knew we could figure it out. Let's go!"

Dan pushed back the unruly dark hair that had fallen across his forehead. As he started the car, he said, "Okay. But we've got to stop and tell the sheriff what we're doing. And maybe he's heard something by now."

Erin could hardly contain her impatience to be doing something constructive. She felt certain they had guessed Annette's intentions correctly, and therefore the sheriff wouldn't have any new information for them. Every minute spent in explanations was one more minute of

Abby's ordeal. But she could see by Dan's expression that he was determined to tell Sheriff Danvers their plan before starting off. "Oh, all right," she said, "but let's hurry!"

When they got to the police station, Erin limped inside ahead of Dan. But Sheriff Danvers wasn't there. The officer on duty explained that the sheriff had been called out to a fire of suspicious origin and had no idea when he'd be back.

Dan said to him, "We're the people who reported a child missing—Abby Peters. Is there any news about her?"

The officer shook his head. "Nope. Sheriff made a lot of calls, but nothing's come in on it yet." He glanced at Dan and added, "Sorry. You kids want to wait and see if anything shows up?"

Drumming her fingers on the counter, Erin listened as Dan replied slowly, "Well, no, I guess not. But I'd like to leave a message for the sheriff. Will you tell him—" He paused so long that Erin thought she'd scream in frustration. "Tell him Dan Peters, that's me, had an idea about where to look for my half-sister. But I'm not exactly sure where the place is—I'll have to try and find it. Anyway, it's called Stoner House and it's in New York State." Seeing that the officer had jotted all this down,

Dan added, "Tell the sheriff I'll give him a call later on."

Erin was already waiting at the door while Dan thanked the policeman and turned to leave. Once back in the car, she sighed with relief as he nosed the Ford out onto the highway.

Racing through the night, the car's high beams made a tunnel of light along the pitch-dark country road. Erin watched for the highway signs, consulting her map, and gave Dan directions for each turn on the way to High River. In another part of her mind, she was repeating over and over like a litany, "Hang on, Abby, we're coming! Hang on, Abby, we're coming!" The child's teddy bear, waiting patiently in the back seat, was the one symbol of hope Erin could cling to.

Dan hardly spoke except to mutter, "Come on, you jerk, get a move on!" to slow-moving vehicles in front of them and to grunt an acknowledgement of Erin's instructions. She glanced at him from time to time and saw his square jaw set in grim determination. He's someone I can truly rely on, she thought with a rush of gratitude. He won't give up until we've seen this through to the end.

They passed through the sleepy little village of High River. "It won't be long now," she told him. "Does anything look familiar?"

"Not yet." But five miles later he braked

abruptly and then turned right on a small unmarked road. "I remember that sign—Jackrabbit's Hole. Weird name for a restaurant."

Erin leaned back in her seat. It was up to Dan now, and he was concentrating fiercely, waiting for landmarks to jog his memory of that long-ago trip. There was nothing more she could do—she'd have to wait and hope that his sense of direction would lead them to Stoner House.

Staring at the black road unrolling ahead of the car's lights, Erin couldn't keep her mind from asking the same futile questions. Would Abby be at Stoner House when they finally found it? What was the little girl thinking and feeling right now? Was she scared, hungry, hurt? And what would happen when they found her? Erin's heart pounded as she remembered Annette's hysterical voice on the phone. Would this desperate woman let them take her child away? Thank God Dan is here, too, she thought. His strength buoyed up her own courage, and maybe he could find the words to persuade Annette to release Abby.

With a start Erin realized that the car was coasting quietly to a stop. A pair of stone gate-posts marked the beginning of a winding road, rutted and sprouting with weeds. "This is it," Dan told her. And as she gazed at the stone pillars, she saw a brass plate blackened with age and half hidden by ivy. The letters read ''Sto   H se.''

She stifled a gasp as Dan turned into the drive. We're really here—we found it, she thought. The full meaning of what they were doing hit Erin like a shock of cold water, and for a moment she wanted to turn and run away. But you can't, she told herself sternly. You have a responsibility to Abby, and to yourself.

The car stopped once more beside the old gatehouse. Dan had already turned off the car's headlights, and now he took the lantern from the floor beside Erin. When he directed its beam onto the gatehouse door, both of them could see it had not been disturbed for many years. The padlock was rusted shut and tangled cobwebs stretched across the top of the doorway.

Satisfied, Dan switched off the light. Slipping the car into gear, he crept carefully up the bumpy driveway. Without the headlights, there was only a sliver of new moon to show the way, and once they startled a fat raccoon waddling across in front of them.

Around the final curve, Stoner House loomed before them, a massive structure that even in the faint light showed signs of decay. Several windows on the ground floor were boarded up, and a heap of fallen shingles showed where a tree had smashed in part of the roof.

There were no signs of life anywhere. But as Dan edged the Ford quietly around the side of the huge house, they saw the distinctive shape of a Volvo standing in the middle of the courtyard. Erin clutched Dan's arm and whispered, "She's here! That must be Annette's car."

He nodded and pulled the Ford across the courtyard entrance. "Whoever it belongs to, they're not driving out of here now." Shutting off the engine, he picked up the flashlight and looked solemnly at Erin. "Let's go and find Abby."

Careful not to slam the doors, they got out of the car and picked their way noiselessly toward the side portico. Erin felt Dan reach for her hand as they climbed the three wide steps to the glass doors. At the top they paused. Then Erin put her hand on the wrought-iron handle, and felt the door open under her touch. Her heart leaped to her throat as she stepped inside.

Stopping for a moment to listen, they could hear nothing but faint scratching noises. There must be mice, Erin thought with a shiver of distaste. Then Dan switched on the battery lantern and swept its beam around the walls.

It must once have been a beautiful room, with its sculptured moldings and tall graceful windows. But now the hardwood floor was scratched and discolored, and the paneling on the walls was warped and peeling away in places. A few large pieces of furniture were shrouded in dust sheets, making ghostly shapes in the shadowy corners. There were no signs of human life at all. If I hadn't seen that car outside, Erin thought, I'd swear nobody had set foot in here for years.

"Come on," Dan whispered in her ear. "They've got to be here someplace." Gently opening the door on the far side of the big room, they found themselves in the main entrance hall. More doors opened off it in all directions. But by the time they had looked into each of the rooms, they were certain that no one was hiding on the ground floor.

Dan gestured toward the wide curving staircase that beckoned them toward the dark rooms above. They began to climb as quietly as they could. The pain in Erin's ankle had subsided to a dull ache, but still she briefly grasped the banister for support. Her hand came away covered with dust. Wiping it quickly against her jeans, she glanced at the rail and then clutched at Dan's arm. With a trembling finger she pointed to the smears in the dust farther along the banister where she hadn't yet touched it.

Following her gaze, Dan nodded and then

silently indicated the upper floor with a thrust of his chin. He grasped her hand tightly, and together they made their way to the top of the stairs.

Here, too, many doors opened off a central hallway. Cautiously they searched one room after the other. Some were completely empty, while others held one or two pieces of sheeted furniture, and the watery moonlight cast weird shadows through the dusty windows.

A short corridor behind one door led to a group of rooms that Erin guessed must have been the servants' quarters. Peering cautiously into a small bedroom, Erin felt a cold breeze. Then she realized that this was where the roof had caved in. The ceiling was open to the clear night sky and a puddle of rainwater had collected on the warped floorboards.

Standing again by the main stairwell, Erin felt the beginnings of panic. She'd been so sure Abby was here! But so far they'd found no sign of anyone's presence—just those faint streaks on the dusty stair rail, and who knew when those had been made? But that car in the courtyard. It must mean that someone is here, she thought. Not necessarily inside, though. Maybe it belongs to a couple of teenagers who are out in the woods necking. For all we know, this is the local spot for lovers.

She looked despairingly at Dan, and then suddenly stiffened. What was that noise? He had heard it, too, and they both stood immobilized. There it was again, and this time they knew it was the murmuring of a human voice.

The sound was coming from somewhere above them—there must be another staircase. Erin's eyes met Dan's and with no need for further communication, they started back through the rooms they had just searched. At last, behind a door they'd assumed led to a closet, they discovered a steep narrow flight of stairs.

They could hear the voice more clearly now, though it was still impossible to make out the words. Pushing Erin behind him, Dan started up the staircase, and Erin crept silently at his heels.

At the top they halted, straining to hear the voice again. They were standing at the end of a narrow passageway, with three doors at intervals along one side. At the end was an old-fashioned bathroom, its entrance marked by a set of broken hinges.

They stole along the hallway, listening at each door, and at the last one they heard a woman's voice. Erin's blood froze and she covered her mouth with one hand to keep from crying out. "Now, Annette, you've been a very naughty girl. We can't have that, you know, not in this house. I'm afraid you're going to have to be punished."

It was Annette talking! Erin recognized her voice. But who was she speaking to, the person she called Annette? The answer to Erin's question came in a moment, and a tremor of revulsion ran through her as she heard the thin falsetto reply, still unmistakably Annette. Dan put his arm around her, pulling her close, and she felt his heart pounding in horror as they listened.

"Oh, no, please don't! I won't do it ever again, I promise. Please don't be mad at me, don't lock me up. I'm sorry, really I am."

Oh, my God. Erin could hardly breathe as disjointed thoughts tumbled through her head— pathetic, creepy, sick. She's talking to *herself*— it's so horrible! And what has she done with Abby? Dan, this can't be true! She nearly spoke the words aloud and her arm tightened around his waist.

Dan silently pushed the door open and they stood watching in the doorway as Annette spoke again in her grown-up voice. "That's not enough. Anyone can say they're sorry. Little girls who do bad things have to be punished, and we know Annette has been very bad."

Erin tore her eyes away from the gaunt figure

of the woman by the window. There was Abby! The child was scrunched up against the head of a big iron bedstead, her face puckered with fear. One thumb was in her mouth, and then Erin saw that her other arm was tied by the wrist to the bed. "My God! Abby!" Erin cried out as she rushed to the child.

Annette's head jerked up. "No, I didn't mean it!" she wailed in her little-girl voice. "I don't want to be punished anymore. I'll be good, I promise!"

Dan walked slowly toward Annette, holding out his hands in a gesture of comfort and understanding. But Annette scrambled up on the wide window ledge and pushed open the hinged casement window. "No, no, I'll never do anything bad again. Mommy, please don't be mad!" Her voice rose to a shriek.

Before Dan could reach her side, she had crawled out onto the windowsill and grabbed hold of the drainpipe that ran down the side of the house. For a moment she hung suspended there, but then the rusted metal gave way. The ancient drainpipe tore away from the house with a screeching noise and Annette fell with it to the flagstones three floors below.

Dan leaned out over the windowsill, looking down at the wreckage that lay in the shadow of the old house. He turned away slowly and came to the bed where Erin rocked the child in her arms. "Erin? Abby? Are you okay?" His voice was husky and when he bent to encircle them both in his strong arms, Erin could feel the tears on his face.

CHAPTER THIRTEEN

Erin collapsed on the couch in the Peters' living room in Wentworth. They were all safe at last and she felt the tension of the past few days beginning to slowly drain away. Her whole body ached as the hard knots of fear loosened in the muscles of her neck and back. She was exhausted, but she knew she couldn't sleep yet. Too much had happened and her mind was still running in high gear.

The events of the previous night after Annette's tragic accident were a confused blur. Erin remembered the somber look on Dan's face when he'd come back from the terrace where Annette's body lay. They'd both felt sure she was dead—no one could have survived that fall—but the finality of certain knowledge had affected them both. Erin had struggled to keep her trembling under control as they carried Abby to the car. The child had not cried or spoken a single word since they'd found her. But when she saw her teddy bear, she burst into tears. Clasping it to her, Abby had sat on Erin's lap and through the rest of the night she'd clung to the older girl, unwilling to let go for even a moment.

They'd managed to find a police station and when they'd told their story, there were innumerable phone calls to be made. Then Dan had gone back to Stoner House with the local police. Erin shuddered. She couldn't have made herself return to that place, and she was grateful that she and Abby had been allowed to stay in the brightly lit station house. The officer on duty had offered Erin a cup of tea and had found a blanket to wrap around them, because Erin couldn't stop shivering.

She must have dozed on and off. Erin could remember Sheriff Danvers appearing in the police station at one point. And then, it seemed hours later, Dan was shaking her arm and saying, "Come on, Erin, we're going back to the cabin."

"These kids are dead on their feet," she heard the sheriff say. Then she and Dan were sitting in the back seat of the Ford station wagon, while one of Sheriff Danvers's deputies drove them home.

Worn out, she had leaned against Dan's solid body while his arm went around her shoulder with reassuring strength. Abby lay across both their laps, holding Erin's hand with one of her own and clutching her bear with the other.

She guessed that Sheriff Danvers must have followed in his car. When they reached the cabin, she stumbled inside with Abby and the two of them huddled in the big bed where Abby had napped—had it only been twelve hours earlier? During what remained of the night the little girl slept fitfully, startling herself awake with her own cries from time to time.

In the morning, bleary-eyed, Erin was making some breakfast for the three of them when Sheriff Danvers stopped by. She was touched by his kindness and his obvious concern for Abby. "My wife sent you a pie from yesterday's baking," he said, handing it to Erin. "She was afraid you didn't have anything to eat here. I hope the little girl likes apple pie."

Still clingy and shy of strangers, Abby looked at Erin. "Do you want some now?" Erin asked her and when the child nodded, she cut pieces for everyone.

"I really stopped by to tell you that we've gotten in touch with your father," Sheriff Danvers told Dan. "He's at home, in Wentworth."

"Oh, good," Erin breathed.

"Yes. He'll be coming up here as soon as he can—should be here by noon or maybe a little later. I talked to him just after he got home from the airport this morning and explained the whole business to him. Anyway, I thought it would relieve your minds to know he's on his way."

For the rest of the morning, Erin played quietly with Abby and sat with her while she napped for a short while. Soon after noon a rental car pulled into the turnaround in front of the cabin. Abby heard it at the same time Erin did and she ran to look out the window. "It's my dad!" Flying out the door, she raced toward him and hurled herself into his arms. "Oh, Daddy, I didn't want to go with Mommy but she made me!"

Scooping her up in his arms, the tall man held her close. "Shh, it's all right now," he said softly. "Everything's going to be all right."

Erin could see that Mr. Peters could hardly bear to tear himself away from his daughter when he left with Dan and the sheriff to deal with the grim details surrounding Annette's death. She was vaguely aware that people were coming and going all afternoon, towing the cars to the police station and arranging to have them repaired, then talking to various officials who tried to disturb her and Abby as little as possible.

At last they could leave, and on the way home Erin thought, how different this trip is from my drive up with Abby yesterday. She was no longer afraid, no longer responsible for protecting a helpless child. But so much had happened, Erin could hardly comprehend it all. Now she sat in the Peters' living room while Mr. Peters put his daughter to bed and stayed with her until she fell into an exhausted sleep.

Dan came in from the kitchen and set two mugs of hot chocolate on the table in front of the couch. Then he sat down next to Erin. With a sigh, he propped his feet on the coffee table and leaned back against the cushions. "Rough day, huh?" Then his face flushed. "That was a stupid thing to say. I didn't mean it the way it sounded—I hope you don't think I'm just an insensitive clod."

Erin smiled as she shook her head. It feels good to be able to smile, she thought suddenly. For a while I wondered if I'd ever want to again.

She heard Mr. Peters coming down the stairs. When he walked into the room and stood for a moment looking at them, she thought, he looks exhausted, too.

He sat down heavily in the armchair across from them. "I just want to tell you both, I'm really grateful for everything you did. I don't know what would have happened if—'' He broke off for a moment. ''Anyway, I know it was a terrible experience for everyone, but I'm proud of the way you handled it.'' Looking at Erin, he went on, ''Please believe me, I had no idea that anything like this could happen. If I had, of course I'd never have left you alone here with Abby. And now that it's over, I feel I owe both of you an explanation—or as much of one as we'll ever have.''

Taking a deep breath, he began, ''When I met Annette, she was such a sweet person, naive and almost childlike in many ways. She had been brought up by her grandparents after her mother and father were killed in a boating accident. She had a very over-protected childhood and was never allowed to be independent and do things on her own. But when we married I believed she was ready to grow up and become her own person.''

Mr. Peters rubbed his eyes wearily. ''We were happy together those first couple of years. But when Abby was born, instead of becoming more mature, Annette grew more and more childish. She didn't know how to take care of a baby, and when Abby cried, she got angry, even hysterical sometimes. I guess she was terrified of being a mother herself, rather than the child she'd always been. I tried to help her. But then one day I walked in to find her screaming at Abby and shaking her by the shoulders.'' He stopped, unable to go on.

Shuddering, Erin thought, no wonder Abby woke up with nightmares. How terrible to be afraid of your own mother.

Finally Mr. Peters said quietly, "I tried everything I knew to help her, but Annette just couldn't stand the frustration of coping with a young child." He glanced at his son. "It was an awful time for all of us, and I guess I didn't have much energy to spare for you. I regret that now, Dan."

Dan looked directly at his father. "I wish I'd known what was going on," he said. "It seemed to me you just packed me off to boarding school because you didn't want me around."

Mr. Peters shook his head. "No, it wasn't like that. I thought you'd be better off away from us until things were straightened out. You'd had enough problems when Eileen died." Determined to finish the story, he continued, "After several months of therapy, Annette began to tell me a little about her own childhood. Her grandparents were rigid, unforgiving people who expected far too much from her and then became angry when she didn't measure up to their impossible standards."

Dan's father gazed at them earnestly. "Finally I felt that something had to be done. I couldn't let my daughter suffer for her mother's problems. Abby was so fearful of making Annette angry and I saw her shrinking more and more into a shell. So at that point we agreed to separate and I had custody of Abby. I thought Annette had accepted this arrangement. Perhaps we'll never know what triggered her sudden need to take Abby back.'' He took a deep breath. ''What happened to Annette was terrible, but I know there was nothing more anyone could do to help her—we had all tried everything we knew how to do. I only hope that Abby will survive this without permanent scars and that she'll grow up to be a whole person.''

There was silence when he'd finished speaking. What a terrible life Annette must have had, Erin thought with a pang of sorrow. She'd been so beautiful to look at—who could have guessed how troubled she'd been underneath? She must have hated herself for terrifying her own child and for being unable to stop her destructive anger. A tremor of sadness engulfed Erin. Life was sometimes so unfair.

Then a new thought struck her. All the unexplained things that had happened in this house while she was here with Abby must have been Annette's doing. The phone calls when no one spoke, the photo of Abby and her father that had been destroyed—they all made sense as the beginning of a sequence of events that had ended in Annette's kidnapping Abby and her flight to her own childhood home. Was it all planned out in her head? Erin wondered. Or was Annette so disturbed that she didn't have any idea what she was doing? There was no way to know for sure.

Mr. Peters raised his head slowly. "Erin, I hope you understand how grateful I am that you were here. I know it was really an ordeal for you, but at least Abby had someone she could trust. And if you and Dan hadn't figured out where Annette had taken her, I hate to think how much worse it might have been. If only I'd realized—"

"Don't blame yourself, Dad." Dan spoke quietly but firmly. "You did everything you could to help Annette. There was no way you could guess she'd go so far out of control."

"Thanks, son." Mr. Peters tried for a smile that didn't quite work. Erin thought, it will be a long time before he can forgive himself and put this behind him.

Aloud she said, "Well, I'd better go on home—it's getting late." Wearily she got to her feet.

Grabbing her hand, Dan pulled her back down on the couch. "Don't be silly!"

At the same time Mr. Peters said, "No, no,

what are you thinking of? After all you've been through, I can't let you go home to an empty house. You'll stay here until your parents get back—that is, if you're willing to.'' His smile was genuine this time. ''What could I say to Abby if she woke up in the morning and you weren't here?''

''Well . . .'' She saw he really meant it. ''All right.''

''Good.'' He smothered a yawn. ''If you kids will excuse me, I've got to get to bed. I'm still suffering from jet lag.'' He walked toward the stairs. ''Thanks again for everything you did.''

Dan and Erin sat in silence together on the couch. Overhead they could hear Mr. Peters's footsteps as he walked into Abby's room and paused for a moment. Erin knew he was checking to make sure his daughter was sleeping soundly.

''Your dad is really a good person,'' she said to Dan.

He smiled at her. ''Sure he is. He takes after me, hadn't you noticed?''

''Of course,'' she said, smiling back at him. Then her expression grew serious. ''Dan, I'm so glad you were there when Abby and I needed you. I don't know what I would have done all by myself—''

His arm slid around her. ''Hey, I just showed

up for the last act. You were doing okay on your own.'' Drawing her closer, he said softly, ''Has anyone told you lately that you're a pretty terrific person?''

''Not lately,'' Erin said, smiling a little.

In answer he tilted her face to his. ''Well, I'm telling you now.'' Then his lips met hers in a warm kiss full of promise.

$7.35